SLATTERY

SLATTERY

A SOFT-BOILED DETECTIVE

RALPH McINERNY

Five Star • Waterville, Maine

Copyright © 2004 by Ralph McInerny

All rights reserved.

This novel is a work of fiction. Names, characters, places and incidents are either the product of the author's imagination, or, if real, used fictitiously.

No part of this book may be reproduced or transmitted in any form or by any electronic or mechanical means, including photocopying, recording or by any information storage and retrieval system, without the express written permission of the publisher, except where permitted by law.

First Edition
First Printing: June 2004

Published in 2004 in conjunction with
Tekno Books and Ed Gorman.

Set in 11 pt. Plantin.

Printed in the United States on permanent paper. *05/01*

Library of Congress Cataloging-in-Publication Data

McInerny, Ralph M.
    Slattery : a soft-boiled detective / Ralph McInerny.—1st ed.
        p. cm.
    ISBN 1-4104-0188-X (hc : alk. paper)
    1. Detective and mystery stories, American.   2. Private investigators—Fiction.   3. Women detectives—Fiction.
    4. Chicago (Ill.)—Fiction.   I. Title.
    PS3563.A31166S55 2004
    813'.54—dc22   2004043306

SLATTERY

–CONTENTS–

SLATTERY WILL GET YOU NOWHERE

1

I'm Slattery. But call me Ishmael, it's my name. I'm serious. My mother was frightened by a white whale when she was carrying me. My mother, not the whale. I'm lucky she didn't call me Queequeg. Or Dick.

That's what I am. Dick, as in PI. You're not impressed. Neither was Wendell Streeter when the large redhead with the bun in back told me I could go right in. The inner office was like a bowling alley with Streeter's desk way back in the strike zone. Halfway there I said, "I thought this was an emergency."

"I've been running a check on you."

"You hired another PI?"

His head sat on his shoulders like an off-color egg, splotchy, hairless, tilted to one side. His arms were on the desktop, one hand over the other. Splotchy hands too, liver marks.

"You said you'd done work for Nugent."

"I can explain that."

"Coffee?"

It was the redhead, halfway to us, carrying a tray. I sat down, she poured. Streeter waited for her to finish.

"Is that bun real?" I asked her.

"Bun?" said Streeter.

When she handed me my coffee, her back was to him. She rolled her eyes. Dissension in the ranks? I was watching her rhythmic exit, when Streeter began to talk.

"You've got a terrible reputation, Slattery. I'm told it's only a matter of time until you lose your license."

"Everything's only a matter of time. Why did you send for me?"

"I'm looking for someone untrustworthy."

A reputation is all you have in this game and I might have been offended if Streeter's insults didn't sound like compliments. Or at least sound as if I were about to get a job. Maybe if things were going better for me I would have gotten up and gone. Things were about to get worse because I didn't, but it was a while before I realized that.

He had telephoned the night before. I had just stepped out of the shower and was touching up my hair. I hunched my right shoulder to hold the phone and went on working on my roots.

"Slattery," I said.

"The private investigator?"

"Who is this?" I asked, speaking falsetto.

Irate spouses are an occupational hazard. Working on divorces makes you friends and enemies in equal number. The enemies tend to bear grudges. Six months before, I'd gathered evidence for a marriage counselor whose wife, his partner in the business, was spending afternoons convincing a client that he wasn't impotent. I got it all on film and with the evidence in hand he unloaded her and ran away with the judge in family court. The wife's first retaliatory move was delayed and childish. I came out to my car to discover four flat tires. Two days later, I slipped a pizza into the microwave and didn't see the stink bomb already there. I spent the night in a motel. Waking up to the leaping flames outside my window caused by a couple gallons of gasoline set afire was too much. The following afternoon I confronted Dr. Auvarie in her office.

"I think I love you," I said.

"Do I know you?"

"Does the sky know the earth? Does the sun know the shadows?"

"Who are you?"

"Someone fool enough to dream that you could learn to care. One more practical joke and I'll break every bone in your body."

She had a face like a Barbie doll. Her cheeks rounded into pink peaches and plastic teeth were framed by her violet lips.

"Is that a threat?"

"Doubt that the stars are fire, doubt truth to be a liar, but never doubt my love."

"Who said that?"

I looked around. "Aren't we alone?"

"Who are you?"

I lifted my handheld camera and held it to my eye. "Remember?"

She brought her hands together in a clapping motion. Her smile seemed genuine. She pushed the camera aside and kissed me.

"You saved my life."

"Oh well."

"I had to provoke him into a divorce. He thought it would be bad for business."

Her husband, Dr. Seaman. Who ran away with the judge. He had come back of course and now the firm of Auvarie and Seaman was swamped with unhappy spouses.

"Why are you playing tricks on me?"

She dug a longish nail into my side. "I'm not that kind of girl."

At her age she was no kind of girl. But what if she was telling the truth? She was. It turned out that my tormentor was Seaman. A few months with the judge and he hated me for helping him get the goods on his former wife. Auvarie had married the putatively dysfunctional client.

"Why pick on me?" I asked Seaman.

"It makes no sense."

"That's my line."

"I miss my wife."

"Complained the errant rifleman. How can you miss her? You work together all day."

"And at night go home to the judge. I feel I'm being arraigned."

He promised to quit picking on me. His Jeep was in the parking lot of the clinic. I let air out of all four tires.

Last night's caller had been Wendell Streeter, asking me to come to his office, it was an emergency.

"It's my daughter, Slattery," Streeter said now.

He opened the drawer of his desk and slid a large black and white across to me. I had to stop it before it sailed onto the floor. But the girl in the picture stopped me. There are faces that set off music in the brain, that start small drums to beating in the blood. Would her hair have looked as blonde if it had been a color photograph? This was *chiaroscuro,* an art shot.

"Nice," I said.

"She's been missing three months."

"Tell me about her."

He opened the drawer again. This time he brought out a manila folder. He laid it on the desk before him, put his crossed hands over it and leaned toward me.

"She's being held prisoner, Slattery. I want you to free her. I want you to bring her home to me." He dug in his eye with a knuckle. He pushed the folder toward me. "It's all there. Call me."

"Ishmael?"

12

"What?"

"Do you know Herman Melville?"

"Who the hell is he?"

"Another missing person. I'll study this," I said, standing. I slapped the folder against my leg, spilling the contents on the rug. I stooped to gather them up. I walked the length of the office and, at the door, turned. "I'll call you."

The redhead with the bun was named Priscilla. I made a date with her for five-thirty in the lounge of the Bonaventure.

"Can you see Mr. Norris for a few minutes?"

"Norris."

"The firm is Streeter & Norris."

"Ah."

She picked up her phone and spoke into it. "I'll send Slattery in now, Phil."

Phil? She called Streeter Mr. Streeter. I checked her hands again. She wore half a dozen rings but none of them suggested plighted troth or even the proximate intention to plight. Was the date in the Bonaventure unwise nonetheless?

Philip Norris looked like a member of the cast from *The Wizard of Oz*. A munchkin. He got off his chair when I came in and nearly went out of sight behind the desk. He came around it, looking up at me.

"You've talked to Streeter?"

"My name's Slattery."

"I know your name," he said impatiently. "Who do you think recommended you?"

He went back around the desk and climbed into his chair and regained the appearance of an adult.

"He told you his daughter is missing, didn't he? He told

13

you that she is being held captive."

"What do you do, bug his office?"

"Streeter has no daughter. The only kind of daddy he *is* is a sugar daddy. Lois finally came to her senses and left him. Let it be, Slattery, let it be."

"Then why did you recommend me?"

He smiled despite himself. "I asked around."

"What's that supposed to mean?"

"I figured Lois would be safe if he hired you. But a dog will have his day, Slattery. What if you got lucky? I'll pay you not to find her."

I shook my head. "Conflict of interest. Streeter just hired me."

"To find Lois. I'll hire you not to find her. Where's the conflict?"

I opened up the manila envelope and took out the black and white. "Is this Lois?"

He had to put on his glasses. He asked to have a closer look. I passed it to him. Tears began to leak from his eyes as he studied the photograph. "She's an angel," he breathed.

"Who is she?"

"My daughter."

2

"They're both nuts," Priscilla said. She held her glass at chin level and was moving the speared olive around with the tip of her tongue. "Nuts about Lois."

We were in a booth in the Bonaventure lounge, sitting in a cone of light that descended from a recessed fixture above our heads.

"Whose daughter is she?"

"She's more Streeter's than Norris's. She came with his

second wife but he never adopted her. Lois." She pursed her lips and inhaled the olive, taking the toothpick on which it was skewered and bringing it forth unloaded. She winced as she chewed. "I hate pimento."

I ordered another round. "Skip the olives." Priscilla emitted a little cry so I amended the order. "Bring her a dish of unpitted olives."

The way to a girl's heart, as it turned out. I asked her to tell me all about Streeter & Norris, the firm. It was her ninth year with them: receptionist, secretary, Jill of all trades. They were in import/export. It sounded like respiration. Breathing in and breathing out. What did they import?

"You name it."

"And they export the same?"

She nodded. Now that that was cleared up, I returned to the topic of Lois.

"What's Norris's claim on her?"

"He says he's her godfather."

"Isn't he?"

Priscilla shrugged. She had broad shoulders and a massive bosom. A shrug was a seismic event. She settled down.

"What is Zeno's Porch?"

I had studied the contents of the folder Streeter had given me, constantly distracted by the beautiful visage of Lois. Finally I turned the photograph over so I could concentrate on the report that had been drawn up by a rival named Nugent. Actually, I had worked for him before setting up as an independent.

"I taught you all you know," Nugent had growled when I told him I was opening my own office.

"And all you know as well. It took an exciting five minutes."

It was a messy parting. He owed me months of back salary. He had totaled my car, and my insurance was one-hundred-dollar deductible.

"I'll see that you lose your license, Slattery."

"What license?"

I left him in a sea of doubt. Of course I had a license. In the Army I had been an MP; when I got out I enlisted in the police academy. On graduation, I applied for a private investigator's license.

"The *tertium quid* between cops and robbers," Brunswick the academy instructor sneered.

"What's that mean?"

"Ever hear of the excluded middle?"

He hadn't made much sense as an instructor either. Nugent was happy to take me in. Why not? I didn't cost him a cent. He, like Brunswick, was angry when I left.

"This town is big enough for both of us," I told him.

I was glad I knew Nugent as I read the report he had prepared for Wendell Streeter. It was barely possible that there was no place called Zeno's Porch for Lois to be held captive in.

"It's like a retreat house," Priscilla said. "A nice place."

"You've been there?"

"Only twice. For weekends."

"Tell me about it."

"Don't laugh."

Priscilla was attracted to Zeno's Porch by the promise of mystical experiences. The brochure did not of course attempt to describe them. The brochure was in the folder Streeter had given to me. *Come Listen to the Silence*, the cover urged.

"Did you hear it?"

"What?"

"The silence."

"You said you wouldn't laugh."

"I'm serious."

She gnawed on an olive and then a pit appeared and she plucked it from her mouth.

Nugent's report said that Lois was in residence at Zeno's Porch. Residence was put in quotation marks. I asked Priscilla if Lois could be at Zeno's Porch.

"Could be? She is."

"Streeter says she's being held prisoner."

Priscilla began to hum, wagging her brows. Her breasts began to sway. Drunk already? And then I realized what tune she was attempting to carry.

"A prisoner of love?"

"Sophos. She has a crush on him."

Sophos, I knew from Nugent's report, was the founder, director and chief priest of Zeno's Porch. Nugent said it was a stork cult. I asked Priscilla about that. She laughed.

"Stoic. *Stoa* means porch."

"Does it?"

"In Greek. Sophos is Greek too. Zeno's Porch is a haven for Stoics."

"What do they do?"

"Go find out."

3

There is a willow grows aslant a brook, which acts as a pointer when you come up the winding road from the highway. The eye alights upon the willow and is drawn irresistibly toward the flat-roofed one-story building, which sat upon the crest of the hill as if it belonged somewhere else on the planet. It was chalk white, the windows were flanked by olive green louvered blinds, the entrance was a shadowy indentation accentuated by stubby shrubs bearing bright red berries.

I came to a stop, turned off the motor and prepared to listen to the silence. But a 747 lowering its cumbersome self toward O'Hare caused the air to reverberate with its roar. I looked up and saw approaching planes stretch into the distance, separated by the interval mandated by air traffic control. Silence?

The drive on which I had approached revealed nothing more than the front of the building. It could have been a false front so far as I yet knew, an Aegean illusion set up on an Illinois hillside on the landing pattern of the busiest airport in the world. Its architecture was out of place. Something was etched over the door reminiscent of fraternity houses on campus, but there were more than three Greek letters.

My arrival seemed to have gone unnoticed and when I got out of the car I had half a mind to roam about a bit, get the lay of the land, see something more than the facade of the place. But before I could set off, the door opened. Out flew a yapping dog, coming right at me, a furious ball of fur with sharp little teeth visible as it barked. Too late I thought of getting back into the car. The little dog was nipping at my pant leg. I kicked out and caught him in the side and abruptly his barking changed to a whine and he slunk away from me. That is when I became aware of the man who had emerged from the doorway.

The whining dog ran cringing to him and the man began to stoop, then stopped. He cocked his head toward the dog but his eyes stayed on me.

"I recognize the voice." His own voice was resonant; he spoke with great distinctness as if he were an elocution instructor.

"He bit me."

He waved his hand and concentrated on the mewling pup.

"Williams," he said, standing erect and nodding agreement with himself. "I'm sure of it."

"No," I said. "Slattery."

"Williams's soul is in that dog. It is the fate he fashioned for himself during his previous life." He shook his head and a look of great pain came over his long, creased face. His thick wavy hair was shot through with grey. Momentarily I toyed with the idea of letting my own grow out. He advanced toward me, his eyes half shut.

"You come with suspicion in your heart. Slattery, you said?"

"Ishmael Slattery."

"An unusual name."

"Are you Sophos?"

He inclined his head slightly.

"I have come for Lois."

His expression changed entirely. He took my arm and spoke in normal if urgent tones. "You've come to take her away?"

"If that is her wish."

"Her wish? It is mine. Have you authority to remove her?"

"Up to a point." Sometimes truth is a weapon.

I had disappointed him. He took me inside, down a hallway with a deep red tile floor and into what could only be called a study. A large desk, the walls lined with books, an odd smell. I sniffed.

"The oil in the lamps."

It wasn't that the house was devoid of electricity. No sooner had I noticed the oil lamps hanging near the fireplace than the pulsing green cursor on the screen of the computer monitor caught my eye. A red light on a surge protector glowed in the dim room.

"Who sent you?"

19

I was confused. Streeter had told me Lois was being held prisoner here but Priscilla said Lois was gaga over Sophos. His reaction suggested that Priscilla's version was the correct one. If she was not being held prisoner, it was difficult to know how I was to earn a fee rescuing her. On the other hand, I might be able to dun Norris for leaving her put. A third possibility was offered me.

"I will pay you twice what you have been offered if you will only take her away from here."

I tried to imagine the blonde in the black and white photograph Streeter had shown me eliciting such a reaction. Streeter's slobbering over her made more sense, as did Norris's ambiguous but protective concern. I decided to play for time.

"Tell me about Zeno's Porch?"

"How much do you know about Stoic philosophy?"

"Why don't you start at the beginning?"

He talked, I listened, don't ask me what it all meant. The name Marcus Aurelius rang a bell, remotely, but Seneca was a town in upstate New York as far as I was concerned, and a tribe of Indians. Sophos shook his head.

"Seneca was born in Spain. His lifetime spans that of Jesus. He corresponded with St. Paul. He was the wisest pagan who ever lived."

Zeno's Porch was founded on the philosophy of Seneca. It fostered a philosophical attitude toward life. Roll with the punches, expect little and avoid disappointment, when age and illness come, check out.

"Suicide?"

"It is demeaning for a rational animal to permit matter to overshadow his reason. Death is certain. One does not rush to meet it, but one must not shun it either."

His voice grew dreamy as he spoke of death as if it were

a destination rather than destruction.

"And come back as a dog?"

"Williams? I warned him to use his time well. He did not. Things will go harder with him as a dog."

"What's the alternative?"

"The astral journey. Does the Dream of Scipio mean anything to you? Of course not. We live in an illiterate age. We imagine that makes us superior." He gestured toward the computer. "An electrified abacus. But what of the soul?"

The question did not call for an answer.

"Now that you're here, I will show you around."

He spoke with reluctance, but he rose and so did I. It was either that or kick the dog again, but the beast had slithered under the desk where she lay regarding me with bright malevolent eyes. Sophos had addressed her as Martha Nussbaum, doubtless her canine name, but I half believed there was a human being inside her, hating me.

4

Lois was enveloped by the toga she wore, which flowed with her movements, now revealing the line of her body and now catching her up in a cloud, as if to conceal her from mortal eyes. In living color she made the black and white photograph obsolete. She was blonde but dumb in neither sense of the term.

"Willard is after the money that will be mine when I turn twenty-five. A month from now."

I managed not to express my surprise. She was at best tolerating me. We had exited the building in the rear, where a paved patio led to steps giving on a garden descending stepwise down the hill.

"Money?"

"My father was determined that my mother would not benefit from his death. Once she remarried, he felt his obligations to her were over and he meant to prevent any future claim on him from her. He made Streeter trustee of my money, and my beneficiary if something should happen to me before then."

"He said you've been kidnapped and are being held here against my will."

A wry smile sufficed as answer to this. "I am out of harm's way here."

"Had Streeter threatened you?"

"The situation was threatening."

"So you have come here."

"I would have come in any case."

Her manner remained chilly. I asked if I could ask her about other things.

She sighed. *"Do ut abeas."*

"Gesundheit."

It surprised a laugh from her. She loved Latin and had from the time she was a child and came upon a copy of *Winnie Ille Pooh*.

"Winnie the Pooh in Latin. I learned to form the words long before I knew what they meant. I felt I was communing with someone I once had been."

She had studied the classics, Greek and Latin, and had written a doctoral dissertation on Seneca. Hence the attraction to Sophos.

"He is Seneca *redivivus*."

We had entered the terraced garden that descended the hill behind the building. I became aware of others in the garden, catching glimpses of them among the greenery. The men obese and aged, their togas looking no more impressive than nighties. The women were bent and brittle, their white

22

hair swept back from faces marked with pain.

"They have come here to die."

In keeping with Seneca's views on suicide, Zeno's Porch offered assisted suicide to those wishing to shuffle off life's mortal coil. I became aware of the way the graveled paths kept leading to urns enshrined in little groves, some raised on plinths, others half buried in the ground. The urns were filled with ashes. This garden was in fact a cemetery.

"I hope that isn't your intention."

She threw back her head when she laughed, lifting her arms and moving them behind her in a swimming motion. The ripe line of her body pressed against the fabric of her toga. She might have been modeling for Nike—the goddess not the tennis shoe.

She was full of life and intent on living it, yet she had an odd indifference to death. This came from her conviction that death was merely an exchange of one body for another. She would never get a better than the one she had. I wondered if she ever thought that she might return as a distempered dog.

"How much money are we talking about?"

"From Daddy? It started at three million."

"Started."

"It grows."

"What happens if something happens to you *after* next month, when you're twenty-five?"

"Phillip Norris replaces Streeter as trustee and heir. I told you my father was determined that my mother would get nothing. If not me, then Wendell Streeter or Phillip Norris."

"What will you do with all that money?"

She turned, causing her toga to swirl and then compose itself about her. Her eyes moved up the terraced garden to the house.

"Something worthwhile."

"How long have you known Sophos?"

"His real name is Riley."

"Really?"

"Riley. Whatever 'real name' means. He taught in a prep school until he got in touch with his real self and discovered who he was."

"Seneca?"

She wrinkled her nose disapprovingly. Or it might have been against the afternoon sun. Above, planes continued to descend toward O'Hare, a statutory space between them, being brought home by air traffic control.

You will wonder why I had waited until afternoon to pay this visit to Zeno's Porch. Priscilla and I had sat over several more drinks in the Bonaventure Lounge and when we finally went in to dinner my taste buds were in no shape to care what I ate. I have no gustatory memories of the meal. Even my tactile memories are dulled. In the manner of such occasions, she became beautiful as the evening progressed, her words seemed witty if not wise, her bejeweled hand was often on my arm, we leaned toward one another as if for support. And oh how we laughed. Finally we went off to her place and sinned together.

When I managed to open my sticky eyes, the place beside me was empty. A note was pinned to the pillow. When I left I put it in my pocket, stumbled out to my car and drove home where fully clothed I collapsed in my own bed and slept the sleep of the unjust.

At the time I was speaking with Lois, my body clock was at midmorning. We returned along the gravel walks among the urns of ashes and elderly candidates to be contents of similar containers. I found it all very depressing and the presence of the lovely Lois did not completely compensate for my mood.

"What does *Reddunt delirum femina, vina virum* mean?" I asked her.

My pronunciation conveyed nothing to her. I handed her the slip of paper.

" 'Wine and woman madden a man.' Where did you come upon that?"

"In a misfortune cookie."

The quotation had been the sole contents of the note Priscilla had pinned to her pillow before leaving that morning. I shook Lois's hand, we might have been making a bet, and moments later was directing my car down the winding driveway to the county road.

My head was all aroar with conflicting information. Wendell Streeter had hired me to rescue his kidnapped and imprisoned daughter. She was not his daughter, she hadn't been kidnapped and while you and I might find Zeno's Porch a prison, it was clear that she did not. His eagerness to retrieve her, given the significance of her approaching birthday, was ominous. It was difficult not to think that Lois felt threatened by her mother's former husband and soon to be former trustee of three million dollars and growing. I resented Streeter's attempt to make me the instrument of his greed. But the fateful birthday would provide Norris rather than Streeter with temptation.

Sophos, *née* Riley, was a puzzler. Presuming he was a charlatan—could anyone sincerely think he was a twentieth century version of a first century pagan?—and given that money is the root of all evil—there is doubtless a Latin adage to that effect—he should be a prime predator and Lois his prey. Yet the roles seemed reversed. He professed to find her a pesky female and urged me to take her away from Zeno's Porch; she had indicated that when she came into her fortune she would lay it at his sandaled feet. As for

Priscilla, I preferred to keep my mind a blank in her regard. Troubling little memories were making forays into consciousness. Ah well, wine and women make a fool of one.

Before its delirious denouement, yesterday had been amazing. I will not pretend that I am run off my feet by clients, but my work, if not rare, is routine and not wildly remunerative. Yesterday I had been hired by Streeter, offered a job by Norris and given to understand by Sophos that he would reward me if only I got the lovely Lois off his premises. A less scrupulous PI would have accepted all three offers. Nugent, for example.

When I compared what I had learned in so short a time with the uninformative account Nugent had provided Streeter, I could not help wonder what my old nemesis was up to. It was time I found out.

5

Like repels like, of course, competitiveness overcoming whatever camaraderie plying the same trade might foster. My dislike for Nugent had a hundred sources, not least being his easy assumption that I was as crooked as he.

"Proximity to sacred things creates indifference. Wallowing in crime lessens one's distaste." He turned over one hand as if QED were stamped on its palm.

"Sure."

"You grasp my meaning?"

He meant that his having become a crooked PI was the result of some law of nature.

I parked behind the building in which he had his office and, eschewing the elevator, took the stairway to the sixth floor. When I came into his office, I found that only Gwen Probst was there. Her hair was the shape of an NFL helmet

26

and the tips of her teeth were visible in repose. When she smiled, teeth and gums became visible, and her eyes behind the contacts sparkled. She was the kind of girl of whom it is said, fatally, that she has a lovely smile. As for the rest, well, one might once have said that she would have been safe in the Navy.

The computer from which she had turned was a frieze of numbers. A hacker of the more endearing sort, Gwen's presence had enabled me to last as long as I had with Nugent. She turned toward the computer and tapped a key that swept from the screen what she had been working on. No doubt she was engaged in cooking the books.

"He's not here."

"I was counting on that. Care to eat?"

"I'm not finished."

"How long will it take?"

Indecision. She raked her lower lip with her teeth.

"I'll give you five minutes," I said, going into Nugent's office. Seated behind the desk, I called out, "How long's he been working for Norris?"

"He's not."

I put my feet on the desk. How I loathed this office. There had been moments when I worked with Nugent that I doubted I was meant to be a private investigator. Perhaps I should return to the police and redeem myself in Brunswick's eyes. But he had laughed when I told him I aspired to be a detective on the force.

"Maybe bunko," he said speculatively, then shook his head. "Naw. Ish, why does everyone want to play Hamlet?"

"I just want to be a detective."

"That's what I mean. You're a natural born patrol officer."

Twenty years tooling around the city streets in a police special, hoping I didn't get shot, pulled forward into the

27

future by the promise of a pension, my work too bland even to excite a decent disgust? Such was the prospect he put before me. No wonder I conceived the dream of becoming a freelance, a solitary figure sallying forth to do battle against iniquity and crime. But now the romantic glow was gone. If I got shot in this line of work, it would be by an irate spouse. Streeter's call held the promise of a new direction. So far it had as many directions as a compass.

There are places possessed by their occupants even in their absence. Nugent's office was empty but he was there. His thoughts hung in the air as palpably as did the fetid odor of cigar smoke. I sat in the chair behind the desk and it tipped backward. It kept on tipping and in a desperate effort to right myself I went backward, ass over teakettle, and landed painfully in the uncarpeted corner. Gwen's upside-down face came into view.

"Ready to go eat?" I asked.

"What are you doing on the floor?"

"Have you ever heard of Stoicism?"

We went to Vitello's where the minestrone is a meal in itself and were served enough spaghetti carbonara for a platoon of Italian prisoners of war. Every customer left with a Styrofoam carton containing at least half an entree.

"Nouvelle cuisine," Gwen said, looking cross-eyed at the heap of pasta that had been put before her.

"No. Italian." Was she playing dumb? I was feeding her to gain the right to question her. Would a meal suffice to make her disloyal to Nugent? Disloyal to Nugent. That would be like snitching on Benedict Arnold.

Her lips and teeth and tongue were incarnadine with red wine when she shed her moral inhibitions and told me all she knew.

"Nothing."

"Who are his current clients?"

"He hasn't had a client for a month and a half."

"I know he wrote a report for Streeter."

"Wendell Streeter?"

"Yes."

"That was just a report."

"For a client."

"If you want to look at it that way. Remember Jaspers? That's my idea of a client."

An austere standard. Jaspers had been the highpoint of Nugent's practice while I was with him. Jaspers' life had been threatened, by telephone, persistently, but he did not know who his caller was. It could be anyone. Unlikely, of course, and Nugent made Jaspers admit it couldn't have been Pope John Paul II, the Secretary General of the United Nations (an obscure fourth-world figure whose name escapes me), millions of others. Jaspers observed that that still left millions.

"Name one."

"My wife."

Call it an oral Rorschach test. Jaspers just blurted it out. Nugent laughed. Mrs. Jaspers was a quadriplegic, totally dependent on Jaspers, filthy rich and helpless. The caller turned out to be her nephew. This occurred to me after Jaspers and his wife were dead and it emerged that the nephew was the sole surviving heir.

"The case I'm on is like that," I said to Gwen.

"At least you're on a case."

From which I deduced that whatever Nugent was working on, it did not fulfill Gwen's expectations of our craft. The fact that I saw similarities between the byzantine ambiguities of what I was now doing and the practices of Nugent was borne out when I arrived home and found

myself convoyed from parking lot to my apartment door by
three uniformed officers. Lieutenant Brunswick sat importantly before my television set.

"Black and white," he growled.

This was not a slur against my discount color set. He
held up the photograph of Lois.

"Where'd you get this?"

"A client."

"You don't have a client."

This was just a way of prying information out of me, of
course, but I rose to the bait. "There you are wrong. My
client is Wendell Streeter."

"Was. Streeter's dead."

6

Priscilla had reported the death of her employer. She was
about to leave for the day and hesitated to interrupt him to
tell him she was going, since the light indicated he was on
the phone. He had been on the phone since she had
brought him in the late lunch he'd ordered from the deli
below.

"I might have just gone home."

Instead she cracked the door and looked in. Even at the
great distance from door to desk, she knew something was
wrong. The phone lay open on the desk, the paper sack
stood open before him and, she noticed as she warily approached, the coffee carton was on the floor, its contents
staining the rug. Streeter, it was clear, was wherever bosses
go when they check out for the last time.

"I didn't even scream."

She picked up the phone and dialed 911. She remembered the number because it was Notre Dame's record for

30

the year. 9-1-1. Brunswick scowled: his wife had left him, he had entered the Church to marry her, illogically he blamed her unfaithfulness on the faith she had lost. Trying to hate Notre Dame was part of his reaction.

Talking with Priscilla came hours after I arrived home to find Brunswick ensconced in my living room. I had not seen Streeter that day. I had been working for him approximately thirty hours. I told Brunswick the story in its broad out-lines: the call from Streeter, the appointment, talking with Norris, the visit to Zeno's Porch to talk to Sophos and Lois, dinner with Gwen. Brunswick drew attention to all this to show Priscilla the kind of account he wanted from her. The great bosom heaved as she inhaled noisily at the mention of Gwen. Brunswick noticed this.

"You know Gwen?"

I said to Brunswick, looking at Priscilla, "I took her to dinner to pump her for information."

"Is that how you do it?" she asked.

I had an urge to stuff a hankie in Priscilla's mouth. Providing a tempting prurient tangent during an investigation is always a mistake. The *National Enquirer* cannot compete with your ordinary cop in curiosity about the loins of others. Brunswick was perfectly capable of wasting the tax-payers' money trying to figure out why this Rubenesque receptionist was pouting like a girl because I had eaten with her counterpart in a firm where I had lately worked.

"What did Streeter die of?"

"Strychnine in his decaffeinated coffee."

Priscilla's eyes met mine. The coffee in question was that from the deli which she had taken in to him. Her mouth opened when Brunswick said that of course they had no way of knowing whether her story that she had not removed the lid from the coffee container was true.

"Who brought the order?" I asked Priscilla.

"She doesn't know," Brunswick said, altering his voice. Was he imitating Priscilla?

"I was in with Mr. Norris when it came. I found it on my desk and took it in to Mr. Streeter."

"Who would want him dead?" Brunswick asked, making a shaving motion against his chin with one of Streeter's business cards.

I excused myself. I had accompanied Brunswick to Priscilla's and the two of them to the offices of Streeter & Norris to find out what I could. Now I wished to slip away.

"You want to take the lady home?" Brunswick asked.

There was no gallant way to refuse. In my car, Priscilla unexpectedly burst out crying. Had I toyed with a neurotic woman and was now about to pay the price? Not at all. Her apparent pique at the mention of Gwen was gone. Tears at the death of her boss seemed somehow fitting, but she was really going at it.

"It's a shock," I offered.

"Oh, I expected it every time I went into that office."

"That he would be dead?"

"He swore me to confidence. His heart was in such bad shape that even surgery was ruled out. He had had angioplasty so many times he said he felt like the Michelin Man." She dabbed at her eyes. "Who is the Michelin Man?"

"You're sure no one else knew?"

"I asked Phil."

"Asked him what?"

"Who the Michelin Man was. He didn't know either."

I counted to ten. Priscilla was certain Lois hadn't known of Streeter's illness either. But all those visits to doctors, the procedures he had undergone, put the thing in the public domain. No one blabs like people in the medical profession. Besides, hospital records are hardly confidential. It was wiser to assume that everyone had known about Streeter's heart. But then why poison him? Time would have widened all wounds, in his case a mortal one. Or a good scare might have been enough to do him in.

As I drove to Zeno's Porch, yawning, wishing I'd gotten some sleep before all this happened, I pondered who might welcome the death of Wendell Streeter. Lois had lost her nemesis, even if it meant only a month of freedom from what she had portrayed as Streeter's acquisitive interest in her capital. Phil Norris was rid of a partner and now became the trustee of the three million and growing Lois possessed. Priscilla had told Brunswick that Norris was on a business trip and she had sent faxes far and wide to alert him to what had happened and tell him to return. Was I surprised or not surprised to find the gnome-like Norris enubilated in a toga made festive with a scarlet border design?

"My heart goes out to you in your grief," I said.

He squinted at me. "All right, I give up."

"This isn't an arrest."

"What the hell are you talking about?" Gravel had worked its way into his sandal and he balanced on one foot as he dug it out: aged boy removing a splinter from his foot. There was a replica of the famous statue in the terraced garden of the dead.

"Your partner has been poisoned."

I would award him an Oscar for the actor best depicting stunned disbelief. Lois took the news with more equanimity.

"It was not a very dignified way to die. He should have come here and prepared for it."

"How do you prepare for death?"

"I never answer sarcastic questions."

"Touchy."

"Do you mean touché?"

"Or not to shay, as the case may be. I find myself among the unemployed. Phillip Norris did not renew his offer that I work for him."

"Doing what?"

"Not rescuing you from here."

"Phillip Norris has come a long way," Lois said.

Apparently Norris had scoffed at Zeno's Porch when he first heard of it, displaying the practical man's disdain for anything lacking quantifiable results in a predictable future. Did he hear time's chariot drawing near?

"What lies beyond?"

Lois stopped and looked out over the valley. "Des Plaines. And O'Hare, of course. This was once a virgin wilderness."

"Who wasn't?"

She made a face. This did nothing to disturb her beauty to which, I realized, I was getting used. Thus do museum guards yawn their way past the treasures of the ages, longing for a saloon, rough talk, advertisements. What else is beauty than a slightly different shaping and arrangement of standard equipment? Thoughts of plain Gwen Probst drove such heresy from my mind.

"No need for you to stay here now," I said.

"More importantly, there is no need to go. To work would be simply to seek distraction; I do not need money."

It seemed an odd twist on the hermit vocation—endowed otherworldliness.

I said, "I've been reading Seneca."

"What do you think?"

"Smug, self-satisfied, self-congratulatory."

She nodded in apparent agreement. I had glanced at a

page or two in the Penguin edition and launched these airy judgments on nothing more.

"That is because you expect a pagan to talk like a Christian. He has the pride of a man who has conquered the flesh."

"How humbling."

"It is an ideal never perfectly achieved."

"Ah. One continues to feel attracted to members of the opposite sex?" I felt I had expressed myself badly. "Like Sophos?"

"You wouldn't understand what I feel for him."

"He wants you out of here."

She smiled. "My presence disturbs him."

"You enjoy that, don't you?"

"Maybe I am meant to be a test for him."

"One you hope he fails."

"Nothing that happens is a failure. It is meant to be."

Hmmm. Sophos was engaged in the ritual of installing an urn of ashes in the little grove prepared for it. The procession was just visible through the yew trees. I had had enough of the ethereal. From my car I telephoned Nugent's office. Gwen answered.

"Is he there?"

"Can you come at once?"

"What's happened?"

"I think he's been poisoned."

7

My professional advice to Gwen was to get the hell out of there. We met at a McDonald's halfway between Zeno's Porch and the late Nugent's office. The scene she had come upon was very much like that Priscilla had discovered when she found Streeter's body.

"Coffee?"

35

"I'll stick with this." She was drinking Diet Coke despite the fact that she was a study in malnutrition.

"I meant was Nugent drinking coffee?"

She nodded.

"Sent in from outside?"

She shook her head. "It must have been the pot I'd left for him."

"But the same contents?"

"I didn't put poison in it, if that's what you mean. Why would I kill Nugent?"

"Don't get me started on that."

For the moment what was needed was an alibi. Nugent's body was stiff when she found it.

"You were doing research," I suggested. "At the newspaper, at the courthouse."

She shook her head. "You sign in and out."

"So where were you?" It suddenly dawned on me that she had discovered Nugent's body, meaning she had been out and come back. "What's wrong?"

"I'd rather not say."

Well, well. "Let me ask you simply this. If you had to tell where you were, would it establish that you couldn't possibly have killed Nugent?"

"All it would prove was that I went away. I could have poisoned the coffee before leaving. If it was the coffee."

"Do you doubt it?"

"You just think that because of Streeter."

I suppose I did. Who would have killed Nugent and why? If he had been run over or shot from a passing car I could imagine it was one of his satisfied customers, but killing him with strychnine in his coffee within twenty-four hours of the similar murder of Wendell Streeter was meant to say something, and I hadn't the faintest idea what it was.

But there was a connection between the two men. Streeter had hired Nugent to do an investigation of Lois. I might have thought Nugent had poisoned a man who had the nerve to replace him, particularly me. But this would have to be a murder-suicide to accommodate such a theory. Besides, as far as I could see, Nugent and Streeter had parted amicably. And Streeter hired me. I remembered something Norris had said.

"What did Nugent have to do with Phillip Norris?"

"He smokes cigars."

I explained that Norris was Streeter's partner.

"How does he look?"

"Up. He's about three feet tall."

Gwen smiled. "Oh, him."

Apparently there had been a longstanding relation between the two. This made me uneasy. Norris's recommendation of me seemed now to have its origin with Nugent, and Nugent would not have intended to do me a favor.

From the McDonald's we went to an all night movie where I fell asleep. Gwen woke me when she had had a sufficiency of entertainment and we drove to a hot sheet motel where as a security precaution I rented a unit, put Gwen in it, and drove home like a zombie. I was trying not to come fully awake so when I hit the sack I would immediately drop off. My parking space is in the garage in the basement of the building. I slammed the door and moved among the concrete pillars toward the steel door that would admit me to the lobby. Just after I passed the second pillar, I was hit from behind, lights went on, then off, and I was dropping as I had dreamed into unconsciousness.

I came to God knows how much later lying on the oily floor of the garage. Before attempting to get up, I lay listening, wondering what had happened. I seemed to be alone. I supported myself against the pillar and looked back the way I had come.

My car was missing.

I tried to think about that, but my head felt so badly, I had to get up to my apartment. There I took four aspirin, stripped to my underwear and got into bed. Did I sleep at all? It was four o'clock when the sound of bells awoke me. I found the phone but that was not it. The door? I tried to ignore it, certain it must eventually stop. When it did not, I pulled on my pants and went to the front door and looked through the peephole. It was Brunswick.

The expression on his face was that of a man with his finger stuck in a bell which he does not intend to remove until the door is opened. I let him in.

"Call your lawyer, Slattery. You're under arrest."

"Couldn't this wait until morning?"

But he was reading my rights to me. He seemed serious. He was, very. Nothing that happened during the next twenty-four hours made him less serious. *Au contraire.*

I was under arrest for the murder of Nugent, whose dead and abused body had been found in my car in the parking lot of the motel into which I had checked Gwen Probst just hours before the time of death. The clerk had looked out to see who I was with and found Gwen so improbable a companion for a bout in such a place that he remembered us both.

"Why would I kill Nugent?" I asked Brunswick, wondering if he would ask me to count the ways.

"I leave motive to the prosecutor."

You and I know that I was innocent, but even I had to concede that Brunswick would have been a damned fool not to suspect me of the murder of a girl I admitted having an assignation with at McDonald's and then—my story—

stashed her in the Triple X Motel for safekeeping, drove home, was hit over the head . . . But you can imagine how all these simple truths sounded to Brunswick.

It got worse. A check of the coffee can at Nugent's office revealed that it was richly laced with strychnine. I had recently visited the office. There is a principle of parsimony in such investigations that demanded that one suspect account for the two deaths Brunswick now had on his hands. If I had killed Nugent, why not Streeter as well?

"Why would I take him out to my car and drive around with him in the trunk?"

"I'll leave that to the psychiatrists."

Even my lawyer treated my story as a lie he would do his hopeless best to make plausible to a jury.

"We can plead insanity," Fisher said, dragging on his cigarette. Jails are the last places on earth that do not have no-smoking areas.

"If this goes on, it may become true."

Fisher looked at the blank sheet of paper before him. "Let's get back to your defense."

"Fisher, I have no motive."

Like Brunswick he dismissed this. I had opportunity, I alone seemed to be a link between the two murders. Maybe I *was* crazy. Had I, unbeknownst to myself, killed two people? Nonsense. I had hated Nugent's guts, but killing people is not one of the things I do. As for Streeter, he represented income. And why would I have involved Gwen Probst by loading the coffee can and then compromising her by taking her to the Triple X with Nugent's body in the trunk? I liked her. In a way unintelligible to the clerk at the Triple X, I loved her. I would not have harmed a hair on her head.

And then Gwen confessed to killing Nugent, stealing my

car and everything. Her effort was met with laughter.

"If only the strychnine hadn't been found in the trunk of your car," Brunswick sighed.

As it turned out, that was what saved me. Gwen did the kind of dog work the police were disinclined to do, having me snug in a cell. She tracked down the sale of the poison and produced a clerk who remembered the buyer. He was certain it had been Nugent. This turned the tables. Gwen also introduced a reporter with bulging eyes that never blinked who wrote a series of stories for a lesser newspaper in which Nugent's ire at being replaced by me as Streeter's PI, added to the stormy nature of our relations when I worked with him, were developed into sufficient motive for a man eaten up by envy. A sensational TV program picked this up, that in turn got it into the mainstream and soon it was received opinion that Nugent had killed Streeter and then himself, contriving to make his suicide look like murder with me the apparent agent.

"It doesn't make a lot of sense."

Poppe, the exophthalmic reporter, didn't blink. But then he had suggested a rivalry between Nugent and me over Gwen.

"Where did he get that?"

"Reporters," Gwen said and shrugged. Her shoulders lifted, her sticklike body seemed to be folding up for storage.

So I was out of the slammer, behind my desk, thinking. Gwen put a cup of coffee before me. I pushed it toward her. "Taste it."

She thought I was serious. Maybe I was. She delicately tasted the brew. She hated coffee. What a girl. If only she had a female body.

"One," I said, "I didn't do it. Two, this was not murder-

suicide. Nugent couldn't shoot himself in the foot without
missing. Three, the only motive that makes sense is the
three million."

She put a fanned hand of travel brochures on the desk.
"I like the Acapulco ones best."

I brushed them aside. "This is a matter of honor, Gwen.
I owe it to my dead client."

"Oh bushwa."

"Gwen, my purpose in life was not to exonerate myself."

"By locating the man who sold the strychnine?"

"That was a good piece of work. I'm grateful." And then
it struck me. "I was a diversion. Who's the real target
here?"

Gwen did not offer a guess.

"Lois," I whispered.

"Oh bushwa."

I ignored her. I sent her on an errand, to the courthouse,
to get photocopies of the marriages and divorces that
formed the tangled background out of which three million
and growing had emerged. I myself arranged to meet
Priscilla in the bar of the Bonaventure. I picked it for its
convenience. She reacted as if it were a sentimental choice.

"Don't try to get me drunk again."

"It was effortless."

"Oh you." She giggled.

Q

Somewhat to my surprise, Phillip Norris was with Priscilla.
The little man had been given several phone books to in-
crease his height so he could look over the table.

"Thanks for visiting me in jail."

"Your lawyer prevented me," Priscilla said.

41

Norris was there to ask me what the chances were that Gwen had killed Streeter and Nugent. "She sounded pretty plausible to me." He had heard her confession on TV.

"Why would she do it?"

Priscilla said, "That's why Phil wanted to come along."

"I liked you better in a toga."

The import/export entrepreneur paused as if to let the pain subside. "It's about Zeno's Porch that I have come to speak."

He said he appreciated my surprise at finding him there. Direct action had seemed called for in the matter of Lois's impending inheritance. With Streeter dead, Norris's trusteeship had begun and, he assured me, he intended to take his responsibilities seriously.

"That charlatan could easily persuade her to sign over her fortune to his absurd operation."

"Now, Phil," Priscilla said in a wheedling voice.

"If he isn't a fraud, I am a nine-foot giant."

I laughed. I couldn't help myself. Once more Norris waited me out. He went on. He made a plausible case, the obvious case. Sophos was a sophist interested in power, money and self-indulgent pleasure. More or less in that order. Professing to be disinterested in Lois, asking me to take her away, could be merely a shrewd move. I told Norris of it. He snorted.

"Is that why I came upon them in a clinch behind a juniper tree?" he growled.

"*In flagrante delicto?*" Priscilla asked.

"No, in the garden."

Absent from his theory was any explanation of the deaths of Streeter and Nugent. I complained about this.

"They're explained. Nugent bought the strychnine. Slattery, I want you to get the goods on Sophos." He slapped an envelope on the table. I raised the flap. A check. I shook my head.

"Cash."

He agreed and on the strength of that I agreed, and then Norris left me with Priscilla.

"It was nice of the Probst girl to try to save you."

"Yeah."

"You used to work together?"

I found that I was embarrassed to have this middle-aged charmer connect me with Gwen Probst. It was not simply that Gwen left my concupiscence unaddressed whereas Priscilla absurdly did not. More absurdly still, there was a rivalry between Gwen and myself. Oh yes. I had felt it from the first. Gwen, unconsciously I am sure, resented the subservient, gopher role Nugent cast her for. She had been with him several years when I joined the agency. To say she knew as much as Nugent is not to say much. I found myself brooding on this when Priscilla, lips moist with martini, suggested that we adjourn to her place.

"I'll put something in the oven," she breathed, pressing her knee to mine.

"Give me a rain check."

"It's not raining."

"I've got a headache."

"Oh, you."

Oh me, indeed. But in the billiards of the mind my thoughts had bounced from Streeter to Lois to Norris to Nugent. I turned my car in the direction of Nugent's office. No one was there, but my old key let me in. Two hours later I found what unconsciously I had been seeking. A second report to Streeter. Being careful, I got comfortable in Nugent's chair and read with grudging admiration what he had dug up.

This was first class detective work, no doubt about it. Nothing fancy, no dramatic moves, just dogged pursuit of the obvious. Streeter had given me a quick statement of Lois's parentage. This report tracked back through the marriages and divorces and remarriages that had involved Edwina Maltby prior to her marriage to Wendell Streeter. This woman had been a veritable Chaucerian figure, taking on and discarding husbands with breathtaking rapidity, always trading up, until she was able to write the will that made Lois heir to three million. Not that her marital career had been over at the time, there were three husbands to go, of whom Streeter had been the penultimate. Simply disentangling the spousal strands was an achievement. Out of it emerged a startling fact. The report gave reason to doubt that Lois was indeed the legal daughter of Edwina and this made it doubtful that she fulfilled the description of the heir to be found in Edwina's will. The report first established that Lois was not Edwina's natural child. In fact, she was a child adopted by Edwina's second husband in an earlier marriage. What was lacking was any evidence that Edwina had adopted Lois either during that marriage or at any time afterward. What did it all mean? The report ended with the enigmatic suggestion that a true heir might be in existence.

I was sitting there lost in thought when Gwen came in.

"I thought you left."

"I came back."

"I see that. What are you reading?"

"Obviously you never read this."

She scarcely glanced at the report when I handed it to her. "I wrote it."

I felt a flicker of annoyance. Gwen's manner suggested that the contents of the report were unimportant. Why trouble to spell out its implications for her? If she had typed up this report without appreciating its significance for recent events, why tax her mind now?

I dropped her at the Y where she had a room, dismissing her grinning suggestion that we catch a movie at the Triple X. Apparently the motel had closed-circuit television and pumped entertainment worthy of its name into the units. I needed solitude. I wanted to think. It occurred to me to sign in at Zeno's Porch, where I could both meditate and check out some of the initial implications of Nugent's second report to Streeter.

The receptionist asked me to wait. I sat in a simple but carefully engineered chair and closed my eyes, letting the music engulf me. Is there a more sensual medium than music? Yet it manages to lift the soul free of the body. When I heard my name I was almost surprised that I had ears to hear and eyes to open. Sophos stood there, enveloped in a scarlet cloak. He waited for me to tell him what I had already told the receptionist.

"I would like to stay here for a day or two."

"This is not a motel."

"I can afford it."

"That is not what I meant. Why are you here?"

It was like being called before the principal. Before I had spoken with him on the same level, a nosy intruder against whom he had to defend himself. Now I was a supplicant.

"I feel lost," I began. "I don't know exactly who I am."

"Don't." That was all. Just don't. He said I could stay the night.

"On one condition. That you persuade Lois to leave with you."

Poor Lois. Of course I promised, for whatever good that was. Lois had lost what he must unconsciously think her trump. The ultimate persuasion. Three million plus. I was issued a toga and led off to a room. Spare and Spartan would describe it. A single mattress on a frame that raised it only inches from the floor. No chairs. A straw mat on which to sit, kneel, stand on one's head. The room might have been designed for Phillip Norris. During the first minute I was alone, the dreadful thought struck.

Sophos had renewed his request that I take Lois away. Was it possible that he knew she was not an heiress, that all she had to commend her now was her heart-stopping beauty? This would explain his indifference. It seemed impossible that he could be indifferent to both money and beauty. I felt awful. I felt deprived of the power knowledge confers. Gwen might dismiss or fail to see the significance of the alleged doubtful status of Lois as heir, but Sophos would draw the obvious conclusion. A darker thought came. If Streeter had communicated the contents of the report to Sophos and if Sophos had designs on Lois's money, then the deaths of Nugent and Streeter removed the chance that her inability to inherit would become known. What stood in the way of this line of thought was Sophos's reiterated wish that Lois be removed from the premises.

Clad in my toga, I left my room and the building and gained the terraced garden down whose levels I meditatively descended. On the lowest level, with twilight brightening the beams of landing planes above and turning the greenery of the garden into shadowy clusters, I became aware of voices. A female voice, then a male's, then silence. I moved in the direction I had last heard them. I stopped. Shading my eyes from the landing lights, I grew accustomed to the darkness. I was unobserved. It was the first time I had seen Sophos without a toga. Lois was no longer wearing hers either. They clung to one another as they stood over a sprinkler from which rose a silvery ever-altering aqueous flower; it encompassed them, a species of liquid fig leaf.

Discreetly I withdrew. In that light, you may not have seen the smile on my face. So much for Sophos's alleged indifference to Lois.

9

Why such romping in the out of doors, love among the burial urns? Because the house itself was run on the model of a Trappist monastery, heavy on reminders of mortality, getting ready to die. *Memento mori.* Hanky-pank in such a setting would be doubly unwelcome. Not that I would wish to press the parallel with the Trappists too far.

"Do all these people believe in reincarnation?" I had asked Sophos.

"Oh no. Half the time I don't believe in it myself."

"They just want to die?"

"It's more *vale* than *ave*, yes. Farewell to this life, rather than greetings to another. I encourage such clients to think of it as a redistribution of molecules. Lucretius can act as patron for them."

A pagan sage for all tastes. I suppose some Stoic advocated going out on a wave of venereal excess, but perhaps Sophos thought that would be a hard case to make with the septuagenarians and even older clients who crept about the place getting ready to make the great goodbye. Not that I was troubled any longer by thoughts that Sophos believed all the bunk he preached. Lois and three million plus interest provided explanation enough. And motive. Standing between him and those twin goals had been Wendell Streeter and the unfortunate Nugent. Making public the claims of Nugent's second report would have removed Lois's legal claim to all that money and not even her beauty could compensate for such a loss. At last I had motive. But what of opportunity? I needed more before I went to Brunswick.

Back in my room I shuffled off the mortal toga, dressed for the twentieth century, and left.

Despite the hour, I decided to work out of my office. I phoned Gwen but could not reach her at the Y. On a chance I called Nugent's office and, after half a dozen rings, Gwen answered in a disguised voice.

"Slattery."

"Did Priscilla reach you?"

"No." The nerve of that woman, using Gwen as go-between. It was not beyond Priscilla to suggest that there was something going on between us. With a mind unclouded by alcohol, I could see that for the ridiculous conjunction it was. And it embarrassed me to think that Gwen would think I was susceptible to the aging wiles of the bosomy Jill of all trades at Streeter & Norris.

"I think you should talk with her."

"Yeah."

"Where have you been?"

"Gwen, I think that I have the solution Brunswick has sought in vain."

"The report you found here?"

"That's right. I'm glad you see its significance. Gwen, how many copies of it are there?"

"Printed out? Just this one."

"Did Nugent turn it over to Streeter?"

"He gave him the contents orally. You know what Nugent was like."

At the moment I was grateful for his unwillingness to turn over what a client had paid for when he saw a way of turning it to a greater profit.

"And I have it on my computer."

"Good. That thing is dynamite. You might get that copy out of the office."

"Why did you call?"

"What do we know about the whereabouts of Sophos and Lois when Streeter and Nugent were killed?"

She made an impatient noise. "I wish you'd concentrate on Priscilla."

"Does she know what those two were doing?"

"Nugent's first move was to put tails on everyone. By the time Sophos came into it, he needed extra help."

"Who?"

She hesitated. "Halper?"

Ye gods. If Nugent was several circles down in the hell of private investigation, "Hamburger" Halper would have been in the circle of ice except for the lack of malice. With him it was simply stupidity and an aversion to the good. Anyone who made the mistake of enlisting his services became fitting prey. Like Nugent, he assumed that anyone hiring an investigator was himself a worthy subject of investigation. Customers began by paying a retainer and ended by paying blackmail. Nugent would have used him only because there was honor among thieves. A kind of postponed gratification of the acquisitive impulse on the theory that any present curbing of appetite would lead to bigger bucks in the future. Nugent had put Halper on Sophos!

"What did he dig up?"

"Do you have a fax?"

Minutes later Halper's report was curling out of my machine. I began to read it before the pages were clipped. It was more than I had expected. Halper had followed Sophos to the building which housed Streeter & Norris on the day Streeter was poisoned. Sophos left with Norris and the two men were driven back to Zeno's Porch by Lois. Halper

49

followed them back, stayed on the trail; it was easy duty and he was on Nugent's payroll and he might have been dreaming of ways to extort money out of so prosperous-looking an operation as Zeno's Porch. He was a round-the-clock tail, catnapping his way along. And he was on duty when Sophos slipped away for what had to be the final visit to Nugent. It was eerie reading a report addressed to the victim of the murder.

I looked up Halper and dialed the number and found myself getting mad at an answering machine. "Call me as soon as you get this message, Hamburger, I don't care if it's night or day . . ."

"Yo," an unrecorded voice broke in. "Don't pop a vessel, Ish, I'm here."

"At your office?"

"I work out of my home."

"Where's that?" In the Yellow Pages, there was only the number I had called.

"What's up?"

"You heard about Nugent?"

"Nugent," he said ruminatively, as if the name were unfamiliar.

"He's dead. Your report shows you saw the assailant enter his building."

"Where you at, Ish?"

The question was preface to his proposal that he come to my office. This was a point in a case when a.m. and p.m. have lost their meaning. Now was the time to press forward and wrap it up. How I was going to gain anything other than a citizen's satisfaction from nailing the murderer of Streeter and Nugent was difficult to see. No matter. There was the sheer intellectual satisfaction of finding the truth.

Halper arrived and settled his seedy self on my couch.

He accepted a paper cup of bourbon, tossed it off and immediately handed it back for a refill. His tie looked as if it had been knotted by a hangman, his open suit jacket revealed a shirt pocket stuffed with pencils, pens, slips of paper, cigars. The American flag in his lapel glittered with sequins.

"Tell me all about tailing Sophos."

"Why should I?"

"Good question."

"What's the answer?"

I went around my desk, pulled open a drawer and took out a checkbook. I wrote rapidly, tore the check free and handed it to Halper.

"Is it rubber?"

I consulted my watch. "The bank opens in six hours. I will accompany you there when you cash it."

"Ten thousand dollars." He crooned it as if he were seeking the right tune for the words.

"Sophos," I reminded him.

He folded the check and filed it in his shirt pocket. This loosened his tongue. Not that I wanted him to reiterate what was already in his report.

"Did you wait for Sophos to come out?"

"Naw. I figured Nugent could take it from there."

"He took it all right."

Halper shrugged. I edged up to the fact that what he knew amounted to decisive testimony in a murder case. Two murder cases. Even as we sat there, I called Brunswick, waking him from a deep sleep.

"My office tomorrow at ten, Brunswick. I'll wrap up the Streeter and Nugent killings for you."

"Who is this?"

"Nice try, Brunswick."

"I'm serious. Who is this?"

51

I turned away from Halper and whispered angrily.
"Slattery."

"That's what I thought."

He hung up. I turned back to Halper. "Ten o'clock in the morning. Here."

"After we go to the bank."

"Or before. Right now if I don't get some sleep I'll die."

Halper left and I made my bed on the couch, cutting the blinds, drowning out the sound of traffic already starting up below. With luck I could catch four or five hours of sleep before the ten o'clock meeting. Provided Brunswick showed up. And Hamburger Halper. That uncashed check would bring him and, if it didn't, I had his report. A cushion spring was trying to get intimate with my ear. I rolled over, lay on my back and just like that was asleep.

10

Gwen called at nine, having unsuccessfully tried to reach me at my apartment.

"Did you call Priscilla?" she asked.

"No, but I got hold of Halper."

"You didn't talk to Priscilla."

Priscilla be damned, why this obsession with the large-breasted receptionist? Was this a variation on penis envy?

"I'll bring her with me when I come."

Of course I did not object. There should be an audience for this. Brunswick called as soon as I put down the phone, his manner altered beyond recognition.

"Good work, Slattery. I'll bring Sophos to the meeting, of course. And Lois. Norris too."

It was getting better. And I still had time to rehearse. Brevity is the soul of wit, but suspense had to be provided too. Presentation is everything. How to begin? Call me Ishmael . . .

At ten o'clock, I had a fresh pot of coffee ready. I had shaved with cold water and found it bracing. Perhaps I would make a practice of it. I imagined myself lean and ascetic, bloodstream free of alcohol, clear-eyed nemesis of crime. There would be media coverage, of course. Police reporters would doubtless follow Brunswick to my office. By the time he arrived he would have an entourage.

It was a stern faced Priscilla who showed up first. I offered my cheek for her kiss and she walloped me.

"What's that for?"

"Starters."

She slumped sulking into a chair. A woman scorned? If she embarrassed me in front of the others, I would kill her.

Suddenly the room was filled with people. Brunswick came in and was followed by Sophos escorted by a cop. Lois too was being accorded police protection. From the closet I brought out folding chairs. The general cordiality was a pleasant surprise. Several times Brunswick slapped me on the shoulder. Gwen slipped in, taking a chair next to the cop who sat behind Priscilla. Hamburger Halper looked in, ducked out, came back, then slithered along the back of the room and stood in a corner.

"Shall we begin?" I asked. "I've asked you here to reveal the murderer of Wendell Streeter and of my old friend Nugent." I was careful not to look at Sophos. Suspense, suspense. "First the murder weapon."

"A masterful piece of detective work!" Brunswick sat behind my desk. He waved some papers.

"Strychnine had been purchased by none other than Nugent."

"And delivered to Priscilla," Brunswick broke in. "Let

53

me just read your report, Slattery. Your account is worthy
of its subject." Brunswick let his gaze travel around the
room. He might have been a teacher about to announce
that there had been cheating in the last exam. But his eyes
dropped to the pages he held and he began to read, not
without dramatic overtones. By the time he turned to the
second page, I had lifted my buttocks onto the window
ledge. From time to time I was the recipient of admiring
glances from Brunswick. But he went on.

Whatever ruse Priscilla had used to wangle the poison
from Nugent it had worked. In her desk drawer was a spoon
on which small deposits of strychnine had been found.
This, Brunswick said unctuously, corroborated my hunch.
But there was more. The rubber gloves Priscilla wore while
doctoring Nugent's coffee had been found in a dumpster
behind the building.

"Were my fingerprints in the gloves?" Priscilla demanded,
addressing the question to me!

"As good as. Your scent still clung to them, moreover
they had picked up telltale traces from the contents of the
purse in which you brought them."

"Don't forget the video," Gwen said. "Is that in the report?"

"It's here!" Again Brunswick shook the papers, smiling
an oh-you-rascal smile at me. "Slattery got it all in."

The video, a makeshift security item Nugent had installed,
had captured Priscilla in the very act of putting strychnine
in Nugent's coffee.

"Priscilla, why?" It was Lois and never did voice contain
such anguish.

"To prevent your getting money that doesn't belong to
you!"

"Damn it, shut up," Brunswick cried. "This is Slattery's
moment and I intend to make sure he gets full benefit."

As long as he could read the report, that is. I found that I had concluded from Nugent's second report, not simply that Lois was not the heir, but that a real heir was in existence.

"Who?" It was Philip Norris's voice, though only his forehead was visible.

Priscilla stood and turned. "I did it all for you," she cried, and she opened her arms to Gwen. "You are the legally adopted child and the rightful heir of Edwina's money!"

Pandemonium, not simply at the announcement, but because Gwen fainted, falling like a clothes pole across the lap of the cop beside her. He eased her to the floor, the better to keep an eye on Priscilla. But Priscilla's only thoughts were for Gwen. She pushed her chair aside and knelt beside the unconscious Gwen. A reporter stepped over them, drawn by Brunswick's commanding gesture. I felt Brunswick's arm go round my shoulders as the bulbs went off. Speaking for the record, he kept congratulating me on the help I had been to the department in bringing an indictment against Priscilla for the murders of Streeter and Nugent.

"What made you suspect her?" he asked me, showing his good side to the camera.

"It was no one thing," I managed to say. Gwen was coming to. All I wanted was to get these people out of my office and talk with her.

But I was not to be spared this moment of undeserved glory. Brunswick was describing the report from which he had been reading minutes before. He praised it as a model of investigatory technique as well as summation of the results of an investigation.

"We couldn't keep him on the force," he said, hitting me on the back for the twentieth time. "But he remains an asset to the community, and I mean the peace-keeping community."

Lois came forward and was induced to kiss me for the cameras. "I never cared about the money," she murmured.

"It is no longer an obstacle between us," Sophos said. Like Brunswick he addressed the thrusting microphones and the camera with the light lit.

"You have brought us together," Lois cried.

I thought of the two of them, in the buff in the sprinkler the night before.

"May nothing come between you."

11

"I'm out of a job," Gwen said.

"You're a millionaire."

We were in a booth at McDonald's having the breakfast that tastes like the carton it comes in. My equivocal triumph in bringing Priscilla to justice sat heavily upon me. Was I the only one who knew I had gone into the great showdown prepared to prove that Sophos and Lois had conspired to remove all obstacles to her inheriting that massive amount of money? Nugent had dug up for Streeter facts which jeopardized her status as heiress. It followed as night the day that first Streeter and then Nugent, the messenger, had to be removed.

"The video of Sophos entering Nugent's office might have thrown me off," I said.

"Of course Priscilla sent him."

"Not everyone would understand why he would run errands for her."

Was that awe and admiration swimming in Gwen's eyes as she looked up at me? She sat on the floor at my feet, hugging her knees as if she wished they were mine, savoring my hour of triumph.

"You said you were unemployed."

"I remember how nice it was to work with you when you were with Nugent."

"You helped him with that second report, I suppose."

She spoke carefully. "I typed it up. On the computer."

It was easy to admire her mind, of course, no matter how off-putting that great helmet of hair and stick-figure body. But what the hell, I wasn't proposing marriage.

"We could work together again." I yawned as I said it, the better to make it sound matter of fact. "You could type up things on the computer."

"Or share a shingle."

"Herpes?"

"Partners."

Slattery & Probst? "I was thinking of special assistant."

"What's in a name?"

"Ask my mother."

We shook hands, Slattery and Probst, Ishmael and Gwen. In all but name. But as she said, what's in a name. Call me Ishmael. And say goodbye.

SLATTERY NOT INCLUDED

1

Call me. Please. Ishmael Slattery. I need the work. This need leads me to a shameless pursuit of clients. Ghoulish practices. In a perfect universe, perhaps, work would be equally distributed among the competent and incompetent, but in this one it is very difficult to overcome the memory of a few past mistakes. How amazing that people who have broken major laws or are contemplating doing so demand flawless perfection in an employee.

Let that suffice as fanfare for my attendance at the funeral of Michael Whalen. It was a miserable affair, not more than a dozen people there for the rosary, which was said with a nice balance of speed and reverence by a priest who clearly wanted to be elsewhere. I was right behind him when he bade the widow goodnight.

"I'll see you in church."

He meant for the funeral the following morning. I took Mrs. Whelan's hand, still warm from the priest's, and whispered hoarsely, "He was a good man."

"Michael?"

I had surprised her. I dropped my head as if in sorrow. "God have mercy on his soul, is all I can say."

"Still, what a way to go."

Others, anxious to pay their respects and be on their way, tried to push me aside.

"Ah, well," I said and withdrew my hand, leaving my

card. She looked at it in her gloved hand.

"What's this?"

"If I can ever be of help . . ."

"Private investigator?" She ripped the card in half, arranged the pieces and halved them again. She tried once more but couldn't do it. She let the pieces flutter to the floor. Sequin, the undertaker, scooted forward to pick them up.

"He gave me a business card," the widow of Michael Whelan said in shocked tones.

Sequin had my arm and was leading me away from the bereaved. Those waiting in line glared at me. I lifted my eyes and shook my head. "Poor woman," I murmured.

"What the hell's the idea, Slattery?" Sequin asked when we got to his office. From a deep drawer he took out a bottle of bourbon.

"As the widow said, Sparky, what a way to go."

"Yeah?"

"You know the story?"

"All I know is there wasn't a mark on the body." He touched his glass to mine and then drank. "Except for the bullet hole."

Sequin was a third generation undertaker, raised in lugubrious surroundings. If artists unconsciously see others as possible models, Sequin in his mind's eye saw you laid out on his table being readied for the final viewing.

"Just the one hole in the body?"

"One bullet hole." He was a stickler for accuracy. "What's the story?"

I only knew what I had read in the newspapers and what a visit to the ready room downtown had added to the account. Michael Whelan had offices in a downtown hotel that had been bought by a religious sect with an eye toward using it for get-togethers. The plan hadn't quite jelled, the future use of the hotel was in doubt, and in the meantime Whelan had what once had been the bridal suite for offices. Whether this had involved joining the sect was in doubt, but he was getting a Catholic funeral, so probably not. He had been found in the freight elevator of the hotel where he had lain, it was thought, three days before he was found. Hence the widow's remark.

"They take the bullet out before you got the body?"

"I was the one who discovered he was shot."

"And I'm telling you the story?"

"I just don't want you going back out there and pestering Mrs. Whelan."

"She may need my help."

There are many kinds of laugh—happy ones, insinuating ones, dirty ones, compulsive, infectious—many kinds. Sparky Sequin's laughter was of a kind I particularly dislike. But I let it go. After all, it was his bourbon. And it looked as if he could tell me a thing or two that might be useful in the future.

The future. By this I mean, roughly, the period between now and next week. Beyond that I dare not think. My rent is paid until then. I am owed money by two insurance companies and one woman who had reconciled to her husband and now preferred to forget she had ever hired me to gather evidence of his infidelities.

"Gwen Probst still working with you?"

His laughter had made me wary, but Sparky's question seemed innocent of irony.

"Part-time," I said.

2

"No calls," Gwen said, not even turning from her computer when I came in. Was I reflected in the monitor? More likely she recognized my confident footstep, the aura of authority I carried with me, the sibilant barely audible whistle of a man on his way up. Call this my professional persona.

"Wait till I ask."

"So ask."

"Any calls?"

She rummaged on her table before turning to thrust a paper at me. The *Penny Shopper*, a weekly delivered gratis to the uncaring doorsteps of thousands. It was folded in a special way.

"Your ad."

"What ad?"

I took the paper. The ad was bordered by black lines, making a box around it.

"It looks like a death notice."

"It's meant to prevent one."

The ad announced that Ishmael Slattery was available for private investigations and asserted that I was particularly experienced in troubled marriages, accident claims and overdue bills. I shook my head.

"I am not going to be a bill collector."

"We'll specify you won't have to call on deadbeats yourself."

When I sat, she stood, as if we were on a seesaw. Gwen is not the kind of girl who drives men mad in the sex department but she is a very canny girl. We met when we were both indentured servants of the late Billy Nugent, from whom you could say we both learned the trade. Not that Gwen had a license. She preferred to be the power behind the throne, telling me what to do, the way she had told Nugent what to do, only with him she had been subtle.

"This is an advertising society, Ish. Publicity is everything. It's not what you are but what people think you are.

Everyone advertises now. Lawyers, doctors, accountants, architects . . ."

"Grocers, car repairmen, plumbers."

"What are you, a snob?"

"I meant they can afford it."

"This is already paid for."

"Oh."

This meant that she had paid for it, unless she had floated another of my checks. No, she wouldn't do that. She scolded me for anticipating income in writing checks. The greatest embarrassment about Gwen was that she had money. In fact, she was rich, an heiress. She was embarrassed by this. You and I would be spending our time figuring out ways to spend some of that money and have a good time, maybe go to Europe or wherever, see strange places, including some strange women. Gwen seemed determined to pretend she was as broke as I was. She was one of the very few people who could afford to work for me and the only one willing to. She could have afforded to run a full page ad in the *Tribune* every day of the week but she had enough sense not to do that. She had settled on the *Penny Shopper*.

"Well, at least nobody reads it."

"Don't be so sure."

"I suppose you do."

"Sometimes."

I turned a few pages. There were classified ads. Personals. Anonymous pleas from the lovelorn. An awful thought hit me. I put the paper on my desk. Later I would read those personals to see if maybe Gwen had put one in. Naw. She wouldn't do a thing like that. Why not, you ask? I reply, because she is nuts about me. She knows this, I know this, but we never talk about it. It's too embarrassing. Neither of us deserves the other.

"I heard that Michael Whelan was shot."

"That in the *Penny Shopper*?"

"It was on the radio."

It's why I went to the wake. No point in telling Gwen about that. Just another good idea *gang aglay*. Or is it gung?

Gwen went back to her computer. If I had any records to speak of they would be the best organized in the state. Gwen was a whiz on that computer. If she needed money she could make a very good living that way. Sometimes I thought of taking it up myself, just as something to fall back on during slack periods, but Gwen was not a very good teacher. I tried reading the manuals but they made less sense than she did. Well, you don't have to know how to play the piano to enjoy music.

When the phone rang we both jumped at the strangeness of the sound. I stared at my phone and she stared at hers. I only paid for one but she had rigged up the second one.

"Answer it," I said.

"It'll be about the ad."

That took some of the sting out of the occasion, don't ask me why. But when I answered the phone it was Mrs. Michael Whelan.

"You were at Michael's wake."

"Yes." I had missed the funeral Mass however.

"You gave me your card."

I waited. Maybe she had been brooding about that since it happened and now had the leisure to call and give me proper hell about it.

"It seemed the thing to do," I said finally.

"Why?"

"Tell me why you're calling."

Gwen, on the other phone, nodded approval.

"I want to see you. How do I get to your office?"

"Are you calling from your home?"

"Yes."

"Then I'll come there. I am speaking from a cellular phone."

"Cellular? Are you in jail?"

There are many kinds of laugh. Mine was infectious. "My car phone, Mrs. Whalen. I'll be there in minutes."

Gwen had rolled her eyes heavenward at the turn the conversation had taken. I dropped the phone into its cradle.

"Do you even know where she lives?"

"Look it up, will you?"

She brought the phone book to me and slammed it into my lap, hard. I answered in falsetto. "Thank you."

"You can look it up in the car, while I drive." She cooled off by the time we got downstairs.

"Would you like a car phone, Ish?"

"I don't even have a car."

It had been repossessed. But Gwen had hers, a Cherokee four-wheeler that was hard on the butt but got us around.

3

Pick up any edition of a newspaper and count the crimes reported. Not all of them, just the serious ones. Say just the deaths that do not occur by natural causes, the assumption being that they have been brought about by another human being. Now search the same paper for stories recounting the solution of previous instances of manslaughter, murder and the like. Not many? Very few. Nowhere near the number of murders committed. This is why it was really no surprise that Mrs. Michael Whelan should turn to your humble servant.

The police have far too much to do as it is. No sooner do they get to work on one set of crimes than a new set washes the old set into insignificance. How long can they afford to investigate a death like that of Michael Whelan? If it hadn't have been for Sparky Sequin it might have been passed off as due to natural causes. Sparky said there wasn't another mark on the body but the pathologist had found a cracked skull and consequent concussion. A good clean blow that hadn't even mussed up his hair.

"Of course he was wearing a hat," Sparky said.

"How do you know that?"

"I went over to the hotel and checked out the elevator. The hat was in the hallway on the floor where his office was."

"You didn't dust the place for fingerprints, did you?"

"The place is so dusty it wouldn't have been necessary."

"Any sign of violence? Aside from a bullet in the body and a hat someone had knocked off giving him a concussion?"

"Why do you say it was knocked off?"

"Did I say that?"

"Now if I were you what I would imagine is this. About to enter the elevator, he encountered a voluptuous young lady, took off his hat and bowed, thus baring his pate to his assailant."

"The lady?"

"Or her companion."

"I thought you said the hat cushioned the blow."

"And I would have said it again if you had dreamed up such a scenario."

There are many kinds of laughs, but Sequin seemed to have learned only one of them.

When we arrived at the address I had read from the telephone directory as Gwen drove the Cherokee, she turned off the ignition and pressed the release of her seatbelt. It was the kind that both cinched you at the waist

65

and pulled a strap bar sinister-wise across your chest. There are women for whom the latter might have been an annoyance, or perhaps a titillation for all I know, but Gwen Probst was not among them. No boy was less mammalian than she.

"I'll come in."

"That's not necessary."

"Where would you be if I only did what is necessary?"

When we are alone she affects a coquetry that ill becomes her. Besides, it is demeaning, calling attention to the fact that, even if we had willed otherwise, we did not find one another's body an irresistible magnet. She is a stick figure; I avoid my reflection in mirrors, particularly when I emerge sagging and corpulent from the shower. In my own case I might console myself with the thought that the package does not suggest the contents, but I could not apply this philosophical consolation to Gwen.

"I'll say you're my sister."

"By different mothers."

The widow Whelan was unmistakably bereaved. She wore jeans, a cable knit sweater and her hair was a mess. The can of beer she held threatened to collapse under her possessive grip.

"Slattery," I said. "And this is Probst."

Brown hair over the brow obscured her vision but the beer was a greater impediment to clarity. She stepped back as I advanced, and in a trice Gwen and I were through the door.

"You called," I reminded her. I refused a beer but Gwen accepted. Before I could change my mind Gwen said in whispered explanation, "AA."

"He sounds like a battery."

"No, a Slattery." And, incredibly, the two of them burst

66

into a laughter I shall forego describing. It has been said that making fun of another's name is the lowest form of humor. The Whelan household rocked with this abysmal species of mirth.

Will you think me childish if I record my pique at the fact that throughout this visit Meg Whelan, widow, directed her narrative at Gwen, scarcely acknowledging my presence? Of course the woman was asea on a flood of suds and not to be judged by ordinary standards. Still. But on to what she had to say.

The police had conducted for a day or two a serious investigation into the death of the late Michael Whelan but time's moving hand had turned to fresher outrages, mysteries and conundra. ("We never used them," she assured Gwen, so she had heard me.) The late Michael Whelan was no longer the late news. His widow sensed that, nothing having turned up in those few intense days of investigation, the investigation was effectively over. Hence her call to me.

"Can I afford you?" she asked Gwen.

"Do you have Blue Cross?"

"No, but I have a Purple Heart." Her eyes widened in astonishment at what she had said, there was a dreadful moment of indecision, then the two women rocked once more in demented merriment. The phrase had been her husband's as he made a playful grab at her bosom. The relevance of the phrase had been its invocation when she lamented that, being self-employed, her spouse was not the recipient of medical and other benefits.

"He had no retirement plan," she sobbed.

"Well, someone planned his retirement," Gwen said.

"Nothing but insurance. Mr. Sequin explained the double indemnity clause."

Aha. If an insurance company was involved, the field

could get crowded. Their argument would be that, having hit himself over the head, the unconscious Whelan then shot himself. Motive? To enrich his widow at the expense of the honest bettors in the *pari mutuel* of insurance. If the police investigation ended in ambiguity, the insurance company would make every effort to escape their obligations.

"What exactly did your husband do?"

"He was in education." This turned out to mean that he had preyed on the undeserving poor, extracting small but endless amounts from them in return for programs designed to turn their children into geniuses, insure their financial and social success with the prospect that they would then be able to care for their parents in their old age. Whelan may not have had a retirement plan of his own but he had devised a bogus one for his customers.

"Did it work?"

"Oh he was silver-tongued when he got going. Honestly, he could have sold me a plan. If we had had children." She drew her lower lip between her teeth and began to gnaw on it.

"You said you never used conundra," I reminded her.

"We didn't need them," she said angrily. Nature had made one or both of them sterile so they had no reason to resort to artificial devices to prevent reproducing themselves.

The two women ignored me. Gwen had conceived a bottomless—no metaphor in her case—curiosity about the way Michael Whelan had earned his bread. She couldn't hear enough about it. She wondered if he kept records.

"At his office, I suppose. He was very careful, though." She sipped her beer and added with freshly moistened lips, "The IRS."

It was the old story. The entrepreneur trying to keep something from the predatory grasp of the tax collector. It was a problem I dreamed of having one day myself.

"Do you have a key to his office?"

"Oh no!"

Her reaction could not have been more alarmed if Gwen had asked whether she ever searched her husband's pockets while he slept.

"Will you find out what happened to Michael?"

They faced one another on the couch, and the widow had taken Gwen's hands in both of hers. It was like a little ceremony. Gwen assured her that Slattery and Associates would know no rest until the truth, the whole truth, was known. Well, not everything. No need to spur the IRS into a posthumous outrage.

"The poor woman," I said on the way out to the Cherokee.

"I know. But who else would take her case?"

4

Scott Terrill, who bore an unsettling resemblance to the man who played Superman in the television series—unsettling if you remembered the series—occupied what had once been the hotel manager's office on the first floor of what had once been a hotel. Gwen and I had gone directly to him from the widow Whelan.

"What is your interest?" He removed his glasses and rubbed his eyes. With X-ray vision he would not need those window glass lenses, of course, but rubbing his eyes was inspired, the kind of little detail that had made the series such a hit with kids.

"He is Mr. Slattery's client. Mr. Slattery is a private investigator."

"What are you, his interpreter?"

Pretty good for someone from the planet Zircon, or

whatever it was. I took over.

"What kind of a lease did Michael Whelan have with you?"

"Lease? He had a release. I had given him notice to vacate."

I nodded, as if he were corroborating information I already had. "Why didn't you tell that to the police?"

"It never came up. I needn't explain that I had no reason to want undesirable publicity to be directed on this building. I still have no reason to want that." He looked significantly at me, without effect. If he was Clark Kent, I was Mr. Keene, tracer of lost persons.

When I asked him to tell us of the organization whose erstwhile hotel he wished to protect, he showed no reluctance to discuss sects in the presence of a woman. His was a practiced patter but nonetheless verbose. I shall summarize it succinctly for my purposes here.

That wing of the Episcopal Church which sees itself as Catholic rather than Protestant has been called the High and Dry. The alternative to it is the chuckleheaded dogoodyness at the opposite pole. Mind or matter, as Terrill put it. Charles Atlas, the sainted founder of the group whose spokesman Terrill was, had no wish to lead either a schism or a church within the church. Rather, he conceived of a series of retreats for the faithful which would judiciously combine the extremes dividing the church. It would be heart as an extension of the mind of faith, it would be intellect pulsing with agape.

"I thought it was pronounced a-gápe."

"Only by mouth breathers," Gwen said. "Is Atlas a clergyman?"

"A deacon."

Gwen nodded.

"What's a deacon?"

"I'll explain it later," Gwen said, and to Terrill, "Go on."

Reduced to the status of fly on the wall, I found my interest wandering. I decided to leave the humdrum interviewing to Gwen and employ my mind in a more creative way. To this end, I began to take books from the shelf beside my chair and leaf through them.

"That's Atlas's major work."

"I could tell by the weight."

Gwen listened avidly as Terrill praised Atlas. Religion is a wonderful thing. I hope to return to it when I am old. It is religious believers who give the thing a bad name. It is the good ones who are a pain in the colon. I just knew that Terrill believed everything he said and did everything he believed. And I was prepared to believe that Charles Atlas was the paragon Terrill lauded. But I could not stifle the yawns that came ever more closely together as if I were about to give birth to a twenty-minute nap.

"We'll be checking his office now," Gwen said at last.

"The police spent days on it."

"To what effect?"

They had been searching for clues of the presence of Whelan's assailant, and found none. For Terrill I developed a Spiderman scenario with the killer descending from the roof, swinging in the open window, doing his foul deed and loading the body into the elevator, then departing the same way, up to the roof and away. Could a man be an effective detective if he had not devoted precious years of his youth to poring over comic books?

When we were ascending in the elevator I wished aloud that I had taken the stairway.

"Six floors."

"Feel this thing swaying."

"Foucault's pendulum."

71

I let it go. Gwen has a way of explaining such remarks that makes me glad I received a liberal education. Let the Orientals have math and science, give me literature. And an elevator that does not draw attention to itself. When we got to six, I counted to six slowly before the doors slid open. It would be my luck to be marooned in an elevator with the likes of Gwen Probst. It would be the death of the race.

The key Mrs. Whelan had given us didn't fit the lock so I applied one of the skills I had acquired independently of a liberal education. Inside, while I stood in the middle of the office, eyes closed, trying to commune with the *genius loci,* Gwen picked up the phone and called Terrill.

"Did you change locks on Whelan's door?" She held the phone out to me, as I discovered when Terrill's muffled voice distracted me.

"I forgot about that. I'll be right up."

"That's all right. The door opened."

She put the phone down, sat at the desk, and began shuffling through Whelan's records. As a rule he burned his boats behind him but Gwen was able to reconstruct the last month of the educational salesman's life.

"Six clients," she said. "Could he make a living from only a half dozen sales a month?"

"That can't be all."

"Well, it's some. I say we check out his customers."

Ah, the repentant purchaser of the object of an artificially induced want. I myself once succumbed to the blandishments of a book salesman, actually believing his story that the company wanted to put a set of their encyclopedia on my shelves because of the influence I had on others. That is why I was being offered the set for such a risibly low price. It was expressed in monthly payments that came to far less than I was then spending on cigarettes. The glow went almost as soon as the door closed on the salesman. I realized I would be making monthly payments for five years. I checked the classifieds and found two sets of the encyclopedia for sale at half the price I had agreed to pay. Previous victims? No doubt. Soon I myself was trying to sell my set, throwing good money after bad. Eventually I stored it in a closet, not wanting the constant reminder of my stupidity. Given a chance to kill the salesman, I would have done it as a service to mankind.

"If we don't know them all, why check on any?"

"Did you hear what you just said?"

"Didn't you?"

"Shall we work together or separately?"

"I'd rather keep an eye on you."

"You know as much about interviewing as I do."

That was not of course what I had meant. It took character to drop the matter and let Gwen go on assuming that I hoped to learn my job by watching her in action. I am not an insecure person. I knew the cards were stacked against me, that I had powerful enemies, that in several recent jobs circumstances had conspired to cheat me of success. No matter. They laughed at Edison, and ridiculed Columbus. But I believe in happy endings and remained undaunted by setbacks. Besides, even in the short run, Gwen's misconception of her part in the activities of the firm prevented me from getting bogged down in detail.

But Gwen was reading the list of names she had made.

Morton Selner.

Jane and Wanda Dassel.

B. O. Wolfe.

George Corcoran.

X.

"X?"

"That's all he put down."

"Any address?"

When she did not answer I turned to meet her gaze. "I think this is a joke."

"Why?"

"The address is Gettysburg. 1864 Gettysburg."

5

"How many?" I asked, caressing the deck.

"Three." Gwen put three cards face down on my desk. I smiled. Hers was a desperate request. I slid her three replacements and then, as if thinking of other things, said, "Dealer takes one."

It would have been theatrical to stand pat. I had dealt myself two red Jacks and two red Kings. I discarded a three and got a five in return. No matter. My only regret was that I was not holding this hand in Vegas with the stakes it deserved. Now I could only savor it abstractly, so to say. I bet a nickel. Gwen put a nickel in the pot, then another.

"Raise."

I could have stopped her folly then, but there was a lesson to be given if not a fortune to be won.

"See you," I said. "And raise you . . ." I drawled out the final word, and put a quarter in the pot.

"Call." She flicked a quarter forward with the well bitten nail of an index finger.

It will go well with me in the next world that I did not crow or act otherwise in a triumphalist and odious manner. In silence I turned over my two rubescent pair.

Instead of exasperation, she gave a little cry of joy. No wonder. She held three threes.

"I was afraid of that," I said in an even voice.

Poker is a stupid game but Scrabble was out with Gwen, what with her sponge-like memory and machine-like gift for spelling. Chess? We had played but once and I had retired the game. Call it a fluke and you would undoubtedly be right. Awkward teenagers will from time to time beat the club pro and of course no one questions the pro's superior ability. But I chose not to expose Gwen again to the moral danger of beating me. Perhaps we should play cribbage at this testing time in an investigation when facts mount up while their meaning remains elusive.

We found X at the Gettysburg address. He was seventy-nine years old, illiterate, and thought he had signed up for a program that would teach him how to read.

"Being able to read is the first step," Gwen said carefully. The books, still in their boxes, were stacked in a corner.

"I can read Magyar," the old man said confidingly. "It's English I want to read."

"Magyar," I repeated thoughtfully.

"Does that use the Cyrillic alphabet?" Gwen asked.

Leave it to a woman to say something meant to put her interlocutor at ease. Imagine maneuvering through society at his age, unable to read captioned programs on television, without a clue when personally addressed letters from Ed McMahon arrive.

X did not understand Gwen's question. So much for the Florence Nightingale approach. She had him write for her. Of course it was just the alphabet.

"You should have no trouble with English."

"I came in 1956," he said morosely.

When he wrote out his name, I sympathized with Whelan and all those wags on Ellis Island in the nineteenth century who had playfully changed foreign names to something a Christian could read. In any case, X had not heard

75

of Whelan's death, his inability to read cushioning him from the daily disasters served up by the press. Gwen assured him he would be hearing from the company.

"I can wait. I waited a long time."

His wait was very likely not over, but there was no reason to tell him. Those unopened boxes represented hope and ambition and I was damned if I was going to wrest those from him.

I detected no irony or sarcasm when Jane and Wanda Dassel exclaimed their pleasure at the purchase. They had heard of Whelan's death.

"We saw you at the wake," Jane said to me.

I nodded and observed a moment of silence. We seemed to be commemorating the dead, as indeed we were.

Wanda said, "Mrs. Whelan made a lovely widow."

"I'll tell her you said so."

"Oh we told her ourselves, after she tore up that card you gave her."

It is not good practice to let the interviewee seize the high ground. "Mrs. Whelan is my client," I told the sisters, only they weren't sisters. Wanda had married Jane's brother who had died and the two women had decided to pool resources and live together. Buying Whelan's program had been part of a resolution to cultivate their minds during retirement and old age.

"Not that we ever intended to do the lessons and send them in. We can test one another and move at our own pace. Mr. Whelan gave us permission to do that."

"He was always thinking of others," I said, and in a way, I suppose, that was true.

"Nothing doing there," I said, back in the Cherokee.

Arsenic and Old Lace.

I made a face. "Whelan didn't die of laced tea. He was hit over the head and then shot."

"Do you know where Wanda worked?"

"No."

"Kook's Karate. Out on 48th."

"The parallel?"

It sailed over her head. "Of course. The city is a grid."

I began to whistle. A good thing. It would be inadvisable to meet George Corcoran in anything other than a psychic high. Lugubrious was Gwen's word for him, and after you look it up, I think you will agree. I know I did.

His brows could have made several bald men happy they were so luxuriant. There was lots of hair on the downturned head as well. His resentful gaze blazed through the thicket of his brows.

"I stopped payment. I shipped the goddam things back when they arrived."

"Not what you expected?"

"She ordered them."

The reference was to the woman seated in Corcoran's waiting room. She looked out of place in the room filled with young people getting their overbite corrected and their teeth straightened. She wore a simple washable dress, had reddish hair braided austerely on her head, her hands were in her lap, and she wore a radiant smile. She turned it on Gwen and me when Corcoran let us use a consulting room to talk with her. She was, he had told us, in a manic phase, but it could go at any minute.

"I dread it," he said.

"The poor thing."

He shrugged. "For better or worse. I got worse."

"I meant her," Gwen said.

"Yeah."

Her name was Rose and he made her spend the day at his office so he could keep an eye on her. Her father, Stan Rochester, was Corcoran's partner. Fluoride and dental hygiene may have whipped the problem of tooth decay, but Corcoran and his father-in-law were cleaning up on the proposition that it is a fundamental human right to have a wonderful smile. An expensive right to exercise, perhaps, but they were at the disposal of parents whose hearts were wrenched at the sight of a turned pivot tooth or the suggestion of a row of Indian corn kernels in their child's uneven smile.

"I bought the books because I felt sorry for the man."

"For Whelan?"

She nodded. "Michael Whelan. Oh how that man has suffered."

What baseness would Whelan not have descended to in order to make a sale?

"You knew he was terminally ill."

Gwen said, "I'm surprised he told you."

"Oh, I guessed. I'm psychic when I'm depressed."

"Before or after?"

She beamed at me. "During. I don't care if you're skeptical. He is too of course." "He" was the orthodontist with whom she was toughing out the better and worse.

Whelan had broken down and agreed when she told him she could tell how awful his life was. She described him as actually crying right through the signing of the check.

"How much was it for?"

Gwen's question broke the spell and seemed to have precipitated a reversal of Rose's mood. The interview, it was clear, was over. Corcoran, unaware of how things had gone with Rose, urged us to leave her out of whatever we might still do to discover the true circumstances of Michael Whelan's death.

"I didn't even know him, but I'm sorry he's dead. All right? It's sad and I wish the widow well but I don't want it to make my life any more hell than it already is."

Gwen seemed reluctant to reassure him. I grabbed his upper arm and tugged him close. "Don't worry, Corcoran. And thanks for being so cooperative."

"You can't get blood from a turnip," I said when we were back in the Cherokee.

"That's catchy. Let's move on down the list then. Remember, a rolling stone gathers no moss."

"You run an ad in there and I'm rich."

Sarcasm . . . Smart ass. The fact was her ad in the *Penny Shopper* did pay off, and in a way that would have surprised her if I had told her.

6

The message was on my answering machine. I jotted down a few notes and had erased the message before Gwen came in from her detour past the restroom. We had gone from Corcoran to the address of Morton Selner.

"This can't be right," I said when Gwen turned into the graveled driveway of the county home.

"This is where he lives. According to Whelan's records," she added, more or less crossing her fingers.

The county home looked like it could have figured as a haunted manor in a horror movie. Call it the federal style crossed with southern gothic—a wide front veranda with white columns rising two stories to a porch roof which showed an elongated triangle to the traffic; flanking wings of red brick, louvered blinds flanking the windows, shrubs flanking the showy front steps.

"Quit flanking around."

I must have been thinking aloud. Such places induce a pensive melancholy. Was it some intimation that I would end here, a pauper's grave before I died, a ward of the county for life? Once this had been the county farm but the suburbs had surrounded it, land had been sold off at irresistible prices. One of the politicians who had been in on the deal now lived in the home, in a suite separate from the other inmates, enjoying the fruits of his peculating perfidy. Maybe he could afford to be conned by Whelan, but no one else here could.

"Maybe Morton Selner conned him."

It was clear we had come to the right address when we were shown to Selner's room. Except for one thing, it was exactly what you'd expect a room in the county home to look like. A single bed with a white spread, a small rag rug beside it, a table that wobbled and a chair that might have too, if either of us had dared sit in it. Selner himself sat on the bed and stared at the shade that hung unevenly in a window that gave him an unimpeded view of the interstate highway. The boxes of books were stacked in a corner.

"Why haven't you opened them?"

"I don't have a knife."

The unshaven aide who had accompanied us whispered hoarsely to Gwen. I heard the word "suicide."

"I'll open them for you," I said.

"Can I borrow your knife?"

"Now, Morton," the aide said, a concession. Until now he had referred to Selner as Salty. "When it rains it pours?" He explained. "We call it incontinence. Meaning he wets the bed."

"I'll open them," I said, advancing on the boxes with my Swiss army knife open to what seemed an appropriate blade.

"No!"

"Now Morton."

"Get the goddamn boxes out of here. I'll pee on them if you don't."

The whiskered aide guffawed. "He means it too."

"Why did you buy them?"

"They was a gift, wasn't they, Morton?"

"Why don't you talk to him," Selner shrieked. He had gotten off the bed and was doing a little dance on his prayer rug.

"Gotta go, Salty?"

The old man danced out the door and the aide followed, urging Selner to hurry along, we don't want a mess.

I looked at Gwen and she looked at me. Wordlessly we went out to the Cherokee and drove to the office where, perhaps inspired by the interview, she stopped at the restroom while I went on to the office, took the surprising message and erased it from the machine.

The call had come from B. O. Wolfe. She pronounced my name with a long A but her voice was so sensuous I forgave her. It was urgent that she see me. Clearly there was no need to tell Gwen of this. Besides, we were down to the last name, that of Wolfe, and that made it likely that I could find the opening we had sought in vain with the others on Whelan's little list of clients.

"Any calls?" Gwen asked when she came in. Her entrance must be a bodily memory of a role in a high school play. Imagine at a crucial moment in the action that a door at the back of the stage opens, a woman comes in, carefully shuts the door behind her, then turns to the audience with a wondering look. Gwen has been making that same entrance for years.

"Why don't you check?" Always answer a question with a question, when first you practice to deceive.

She turned on the answering machine and to my surprise

81

there was a message. Not the one I had erased, but another. It was almost as surprising.

"My name is Jack Rochester. I saw your ad in the *Penny Shopper* and would like to talk with you." Followed by a telephone number.

"There!" Gwen cried triumphantly. "What did I tell you? It worked."

"But we just saw him."

"So? The message was left before we talked to him."

"Why didn't he mention it when we were there?"

"Let that be the first question you ask him."

"I ask him?"

She came and sat on my desk, wrapping her full skirt around her legs, as if to save me from temptation. The full skirt was a good idea, concealing her meatless bones, but it did emphasize her thin ankles as they emerged from the swirling dervish of her skirt.

"I have a feeling this is the breakthrough."

"Why don't you talk to him? I have a bit of a headache."

"Headache! He doesn't want to take you to bed."

"No?"

"What's wrong with you?"

"This was your idea, Gwen, the clients of Michael Whelan. I think you deserve to follow through on it."

"That was our idea. But Rochester's call has nothing to do with that. He called before we visited his son-in-law."

"Because he read your ad in the *Penny Shopper*."

"My ad?"

"Don't say that wasn't your idea."

"Okay, but what was the idea? Let people know you're here and they'll flock to your door."

"One phone call?"

"It's a start."

Try as I would, I could not deflect her onto the call from Rochester. We compromised. She agreed to call him and arrange a time to talk with him, I agreed to take part in the interview.

"I'll call you back," Rochester said in muffled tones when he answered. The phone went dead.

Fifteen minutes later, just when the pizza had arrived from Domino's, the phone rang.

"This is Jack Rochester. I can't talk now. I'll come to your office tomorrow at ten. Okay?"

Gwen said okay. I said I was surprised he was free.

"Wednesday," Gwen said. "Doctor's day off."

It was not until after nine that I had a chance to call B. O. Wolfe.

She said, "Do you know Osco's Disco on 3rd?"

"You're pulling my leg."

"Don't rush matters."

"You want to meet at Osco's?"

A pause that seemed to have a meaning all its own. "No. Come here." There was resignation in her voice, and a tremor. For a moment I was fearful of making the appointment. But I did. If Columbus had been timid we might all be speaking Italian.

I advise the squeamish reader to turn a few pages. You will know of those movie notices with a less than inclusive rating which declare: some nudity and adult language? A come on, of course, aimed squarely below the belt where the average slob is presumed to have his brains. Since you have curled up with this story, it is clear that you are not the average slob. No need to cater to your presumed prurient interests to hold you. On the other hand, B. O. Wolfe plays an important part in this story. I should be breaking our unspoken agreement to play fair with you were I to draw a veil of discretion over what was to prove more than a cameo appearance. There was some adult language but no nudity need show its face in this narrative.

"What does B.O. stand for?" I asked.

It was my opening question and it was the equivalent of telling her I was a married man, a protective remark, meant to reject the construction she had obviously put on my willingness to come to her apartment.

She lived in what had once been a factory but was now remodeled into luxury apartments by an ingenious developer. Every room had a river view. The rooms gave on to one another, forming a series. The remodeler had been inspired by the arrangement of rooms in the Spanish haciendas of the southwest. She adjusted her mantilla as she told me. But this was minutes after I arrived.

"Not what you think," she said, taking my hand and drawing me inside. "I know you're old enough to remember the Lifebuoy ad campaign."

I didn't but I laughed knowingly.

"Beryl Olive Wolfe." She held the back of her wrist to her forehead and spoke with closed eyes. "Beryl Olive Wolfe," she repeated in sepulchral tones.

"That explains the B.O."

"I warned you." She prodded me in the ribs with her cigarette holder, and I felt like Hansel being tested by the witch for edibility.

"Your name is Beryl Olive Wolfe."

She winced. "Do you know that some poets have wept over the name their parents gave them?"

"Well, one can bear only so much."

She looked at me speculatively. Everything was in the balance then. But abruptly she took my hand and disconcertedly brought it tightly against her bosom.

"I like you." She said it as if she were prepared to do battle against the hordes who thought otherwise of me.

"I'm glad."

"There you go again."

"You called me about my investigation into the circumstances of the death of Michael Whelan."

"Do people actually talk that way?"

"With their mouths? Yes. I tried the other end but I was always misunderstood."

She threw herself helplessly into my arms. Not to embrace her would have been like refusing to catch a baby tossed from a sinking ship. Hers might be described as the body laugh, it involved all of her. In this too she was like an infant. Toilet training, distinguishing emotions from thought, growing up, makes us less integrated than we were at the beginning when everything was natural. Laughter becomes cerebral, by and large, we laugh with our mouths. Beryl Olive Wolfe used the other end as well, if not exclusively.

"We were having an affair," she said by way of explanation of her call. "He was my lover."

"That's the best way."

She squeezed my hand. "The police either did not learn of this or judged it to be irrelevant. Your investigation promises to be more persistent. You are being paid, I suppose."

"It's my job."

"Then you can be paid not to investigate as well."

As well? There are those who say I do it better. "What do you mean?"

It is always well to have the other party spell out such requests. What she had in mind was paying me more than I was getting from the widow Whelan to drop my inquiries into the death of Michael.

"Did he ever try to sell you anything?"

"He sold himself. In every sense of the term. Everything was a commodity with him."

"Did he ever sell you any books?"

"Of course he did. Come."

She took my hand and led me into the next room, the dining room. That gave onto the kitchen which in turn opened onto a television room. The room was a study in leather. There were two chairs angled toward the massive television set: they might have been upturned hands ready to receive the bodies of potential viewers. The couch was also of leather with great wide arms and huge cushions. Why did I think of the Naked Maja then? It was all too easy to imagine B.O. in the altogether, on display on those tanned and treated animal skins. No books.

But there was a bedroom beyond. It could have been a room in a girl's dorm. Single serviceable bed, dresser, highboy, desk and one wall filled with books. I glanced along the shelves. Most of the titles would be classified by book dealers as metaphysics—a category into which they would not put Aristotle, Plato and Schopenhauer, however. An alternative designation might be the occult. Perhaps this explained the smell of incense I had detected in the leather room. But the books Whelan sold her were also there. Visual answer to my question having been provided, she made to leave the bedroom. I felt safer there. I pulled out the chair and sat at the desk.

"You were having an affair with Whelan?"

"Not in this room. Come."

Beyond was what is no longer called, at least with the same force, a boudoir. If the first bedroom suggested a person out of synch with the B. O. Wolfe who had met me at the door, this bedroom seemed more proportionate to

her character, or lack of it. She would have dragged me
onto the great circular bed if I had not dug in my heels. The
slight struggle had the effect of loosening her gown and
what to my wondering eyes should appear but that which
served Nick Carraway well when, at the end of *Gatsby* he
speaks of the green breast of the new world that awaited the
intrepid voyagers of the seventeenth century.

"I have a headache," I said.

This turned her on, in the laughing way, and the moment
of danger was past. Danger? Yes. Why is it that the average
sensuous male who devotes God knows how much of his
waking hours imagining himself making love to this female
or that, will, when confronted with a compliant companion,
often show reluctance? I favor the answer which takes man
to be the natural initiator if not aggressor in such matters. I
reacted to B.O. in this matter as I would on the dance floor
if she had begun to lead. However graceful the results might
be, something essential would have been taken away. I
began to think less censoriously of Michael Whelan for any
dalliance he might have enjoyed with this wench. She was a
natural force, a Homeric goddess, not so much beyond
good and evil as not yet having acquired the concepts.

7

I had a headache when I left, let's just leave it at that. I felt
used when I walked out to my car. Was I anything more
than a beautiful body to her, a sex object? Was I so much?
Her ardor seemed so indiscriminate, it was difficult to think
of it as personal.

Yes, yes, busy as I was, that occurred to me. Did B.O. consider men on the order of a One Use Only camera, the best
shots recorded in memory, but the instrument disposable,

into the trash? Had Michael Whelan, impressed by her performance, as who would not be—no, I will not go into the sordid details—sought a repeat performance, presumed perhaps that such hijinks could become a habit, little B.O. waiting for him whenever his procreative drive became urgent?

I would put B.O.'s attention span in the sex department somewhat higher than that of the fruit fly. Of course she remembered Michael Whelan and spoke heatedly of him. Much of her life was lived in the imagination, after all.

"I am an artist," she breathed, when I asked what she did. This was early in the session, so I had to rephrase the question.

"Is anything of yours hanging here?"

A sharp jab in my ribs, "Oh you."

So I postponed the inquiry. Later, spent, disheveled and tired, she was more forthcoming.

"I am a writer."

"What have you written?"

"That is what I am seeking to discover. My career is in the larval stage." A swift intake of breath. "Michael said that."

"So you haven't written anything yet?"

"It is all here." She brought her hand to her breast. Since our fingers were entangled, she brought mine along as well. Do not ask for whom the bell tolled. I will say no more.

You will agree that someone intending to write does well to learn how to read first. In that sense, her purchase of Michael Whelan's dubious program made sense. On the other hand, she might have been insulted by the suggestion and, after Whelan had performed his essential biological function, after perhaps he sought to repeat the performance, she grew resentful, she brooded over his audacity in actually selling her so elementary a program, she decided to do away with him.

"Karate," she said, when I asked her if she did anything else for exercise.

"Can you break a two by four with the side of your hand?" I chuckled.

"Yes."

"Are you serious?"

She got out a nice length of wood and proceeded to break it into kindling, making the mandatory shout as she brought her dainty little hand down on it.

"What would a blow like that do to another's head?"

"Like Michael's? It's the first thing I thought. A Black Belt could have done that easily."

"What's that draped over the chair?"

"My black belt."

She began to laugh. I put up a sham defense. Look at it this way, I told myself, this isn't you, this isn't real, this is a unique episode in your life, unrelated both to what has gone before and to what will come after. Thus is the moral law speciously abrogated. But if the sight of her black garter belt inflamed her, I was like the kindling created by her karate chop. In which, I learned, she did indeed have a black belt.

So, yes, this petite little thing could have turned her body into an instrument of death. That would account for the blow on the head, but what about the bullet found in his body?

"This is really why I had to see you."

"Yes?"

"Michael and I entered a pact that we would help the other out if serious illness struck. The thought of just withering away fills me with dread. Michael shared my thought. He promised that he would administer some painless poison to me. He on the other hand, insisted that he wanted to be shot. That is why I bought him the revolver. When I came upon him, mortally wounded, I took the gun and did what I promised to do."

You see that I was well ahead of you all along. Before I had extricated myself from her bower of delights, I had in hand the startling information that (a) B. O. Wolfe, by her own admission had been carrying on a love affair with the deceased—before he died, of course. Maybe she is into necrophilia, but I don't know. In any case it would not be applicable here. (b) She had gone to see Whelan in his office on the fatal day and had found him either dead or dying. Unable to tell if his perfidious heart had indeed stopped beating, she gave him conditional euthanasia. (c) That is, she had put the bullet in the body that Terrill had discovered. The body, not the bullet. Sequin had found that.

"But the gun was never found."

"Oh, I didn't leave it," B.O. cried.

"You took it away?"

"I know I am a sentimental fool, but I wanted something to remember him by. Besides, I had bought the gun for him. If it had been found, if it was learned he had been shot with it, I knew the police must call on me."

She made it sound like a social visit. On the other hand, taking her story at face value, it took a cool and calculating head to take away the pistol lest she be suspected of being the primary cause of his death. No wonder she would want to throw it away, get rid of it. I said this aloud to see if she had indeed escaped suspicion in the matter of the gun.

"Oh, I didn't throw it away. What kind of souvenir would it be if I didn't keep it?"

"You have it?"

"Of course."

"Where?"

She rolled over, reached under the bed, and came back with a smile on her flushed face and a pistol in her hand. I didn't touch it of course. In the kitchen I found a Baggie and I had her drop the pistol in it. She watched me as I sealed it up.

"You're treating it as if it were a piece of evidence."

"I am treating it with the respect we show that which we are about to bury."

"Where?"

"I noticed the large planter on the veranda overlooking the river. Put this there."

At her insistence, we did it together, making a little ceremony of it. I felt that I had been given a second chance to attend Michael Whelan's funeral.

§

Trappists, I am told, no longer keep the strict silence that made them legendary. Too bad. Those of us in the world need the example of the saints to know how truly rotten we are. What Joyce called *agenbite of inwit* assailed me in the wake of my night with B. O. Wolfe. When Gwen called me early the next morning to remind me of Jack Rochester's appointment at ten, I groaned and used the Joycean phrase as explanation.

"Do you still have your headache?"

"That's sort of what the Celtic phrase means."

"It isn't Celtic."

"Of course it is."

"It's Old English."

"You think an Irishman would use an Old English phrase in what is arguably his best book?"

"It is an *oeuvre de jeunesse* and you know it."

91

Gwen was not at her most attractive when she waxed didactic. I was confident she was wrong but in no mood to argue the matter. I should have said "remorse of conscience" in new English and let Gwen in on all I had learned the previous night and—wipe that silly smile off your face. I mean what I had learned about the death of Michael Whelan. Would I have told her if she hadn't made that pedantic correction about what language the phrase was in? How now I wish I had, for reasons which will emerge.

I told her I would meet with Rochester, despite my feeling that the case was as good as closed. The cold light of morning revealed the implausibilities in B.O.'s story. For whatever reason, she had struck Whelan a blow on the head. Then she shot him with the pistol she and I had buried in her planter. Why had she told me all these things? Of course she assumed that, once I undertook the investigation of Whelan's death, I would discover everything. Her story was that she wanted me to know about the gunshot lest I think less of her when I figured it out.

"You must find the one who hit him on the head."

"Oh I will. Never fear."

I felt I had the villain in custody as I said it.

Did she really take me for such a fool? Did she think she could use me, then throw me aside like a squeezed orange, in George Sanders's memorable phrase when Zsa Zsa Gabor divorced him, and that would be an end of it? Her performance had been impressive but I was not an adolescent, willing to lose the world for the few seconds that love in that sense takes. As I settled behind my desk at five minutes short of ten o'clock, a mug of lethally strong coffee before me, it occurred to me for the first time that my knowledge put me in danger, as it had put Michael Whelan in danger. I don't mean that his knowledge of the fact she had killed him made him vulnerable . . . But you know what I mean. I sipped coffee and tried not to think.

The Jack Rochester who showed up promptly at ten was not the happy orthodontist we had met the previous day. He pulled his chair right up to the desk and leaned toward me.

"She didn't do it, Slattery. You've got to leave her out of this."

In the circumstances you will appreciate my reaction to his opening sally. How had he heard of last night? The juxtaposition of his message and B.O.'s on my answering machine made me superstitiously wonder if somehow one message had become aware of the other. Being taped together is, after all, a fairly intimate thing. Ask anyone into bondage. Or bandage. Or badinage. My head did still ache and my conscience accused me. Why didn't I marry Gwen, like a good Trappist, and settle down to a life of indolent happiness, enjoying her wealth, driving away all thought of what might have been?

"What makes you so sure?"

"My God, man. You talked to her long enough. You must see how ill she is. Oh I saw what you both were thinking. Here is the wife, angry that her husband would have made such a stupid purchase for her, deciding to wipe out the man who had sold it to him."

He meant Rose. Good Lord. The mental processes of the layman never cease to amaze me. That that poor manic-depressive could, whether on a high or a low, kill Michael Whelan had never entered my mind, in the words of the song. I told him as much.

"Don't toy with me, Slattery. I have been a dentist for over thirty years."

"Why would I toy with you?"

"You have no suspicions about Rose?"

"In the matter of the death of Michael Whalen, no, of course not. This was a particularly brutal killing, Rochester. It required someone of enormous power." A memory of the petite but agile B. O. Wolfe sent an involuntary tremor through me.

"George?" Rochester asked.

"What about George?"

"Do you think he did it?"

"Do you?"

"I wouldn't blame him if he did. It ought to be a criminal offense, exploiting people like Rose. She can't be held responsible for what she does."

"Too bad she didn't kill him."

"What!"

"She could get off scot free."

"That isn't funny, Slattery."

"You may be right."

Gwen tapped her chin as she listened to my account of the interview with Rochester.

"Good," she said when I was done. "That's most of it."

It turned out that she, funny girl, had bugged the office and had the whole thing on tape. I reminded myself not to make any calls to B.O. through the office phone. Why was it so much more fun to be with Gwen now that I was deceiving her with another woman? Not that she had any right to expect better of me. Still, I knew what I would do if I learned she had spent the night in bed with a man. Offer to represent the man in his effort to collect damages? I jest, of course. This is just my crude way of expressing my thoughts on the improbability of Gwen ever exciting the carnal itch in any male. I speak in confidence of course. It's not a nice thing to make fun of one's partner. Or quasi-partner, as Gwen put it.

"I would have said pseudo-partner."

"It's my Latin against your Greek."

"It sounds like a wrestling match."

"Greco-Roman."

"I'm surprised you know of it."

"Wrestling is my favorite viewing."

Well, well. Male bodies tussling, struggling for advantage. The ancients wrestled nude of course. There is a classic statue in which one wrestler masters his opponent by grabbing his organ. Perhaps Gwen knew of it too. It was sad to think of her curled up in front of the tube, watching wrestling with an ulterior purpose. But then with puberty boys read the Bible for erotic passages. Anything can be abused, including televised wrestling. Did she think of our working together as a kind of match?

"B. O. Wolfe is the only one remaining, Ish."

"There's no need to interview her."

"Her?"

"Just a small blow struck against gender-exclusive language."

"How many women do you know who use initials rather than their names?"

"P. D. James, H. D., A. C. Deucy, etc."

She ignored me. "Should I give her a call?"

"I think you should continue debriefing me on the Rochester interview."

She agreed. We agreed on little concerning the significance of the interview.

"He's trying to throw us off, Gwen. If his daughter's so innocent, why worry about it?"

"Because she's his daughter."

"George Corcoran is that daughter's husband. He has stuck with her through thick and thin. Not many spouses prove so loyal."

"They are the joint heirs of Jack Rochester, who is no spring chicken. He too wishes to reward George's fidelity."

"He can't have much to leave."

"How long has it been since you had your teeth straightened?"

"I decided to let them keep their natural curl."

"He's wallowing in money, money for which he has no particular use. I noticed he said nothing of Mrs. Rochester."

George had told Gwen what a devoted couple the Rochesters had been. They had gone together since their teens, shared all the anxieties and work of getting through dental school, she working while he prepared to make the big bucks later. He wasn't much of a student, getting through by the skin of his teeth, but that didn't matter once he was in practice. A dentist is a dentist is a dentist, as Gertrude Stein repeatedly complained.

"He wanted to retire immediately after his wife's death, but Corcoran talked him out of it."

"Doing nothing could have killed him."

"If you say so. Or he might have met another woman."

"Might be a good idea."

"Not if you're the heir."

"Ah."

Was Gwen suggesting that George Corcoran might indeed have done it, or was she holding out for Jane?

"I want to talk to B. O. Wolfe first."

"Just because her name is on a list."

"Does she work?"

"No."

Gwen slammed down the copy of *War and Peace* she had been holding. "All right, Ish. Out with it. You've already interviewed B. O. Wolfe."

"Why do you say that?"

"Say you haven't."

"I haven't."

"There! Your ears wiggled. Your ears always wiggle when you lie."

"That's silly."

"But true."

Like snoring, it was something on which others are better authorities than oneself. I had two choices, either make a clean breast of it or go on lying. The latter, given Gwen's clear intention to persist, would seriously unanchor my ears. The former, on the other hand, need not be an utterly clean breast. I might just leave breasts and that sort of thing out of it altogether.

"You're right," I said, my decision made. "She called and specifically asked that I meet her alone." Under pretense of smoothing my hair, I covered my telltale ear.

"Alone?"

"Without anyone else."

"Did she specify anyone?"

It would have been cruel to say that B. O. Wolfe didn't know that Gwen existed, I saw that as soon as I said it. But the clear assumption of Gwen's question was that B.O.'s invitation had specifically excluded her. Since the exclusionary proviso was of my own fabrication I felt I had the right to interpret it. It was I who had excluded Gwen and on not altogether scrutable principles. The fact is that I had wanted to score a coup at her expense. Thank God I had. Imagine what she would have made of B.O.'s admission that she had come upon the fallen Whalen and actually put

a bullet into him with a pistol that had been her gift to him
and which she subsequently removed from the scene.

"Did she say what she did with it?"

Gwen's question alerts you to the fact that I brought her
fully up to speed on the essential points of my *tête-à-tête*, to
put it mildly, with B. O. Wolfe.

"Got rid of it."

"Where? In the river? Flung into a field from her
speeding automobile? Put out with the garbage?"

"She buried it."

"Do you believe her?"

"Yes."

She shook her head impatiently. "Well, why not? If you
believe any of it, why not believe it all?"

"Exactly."

"By that point you had established your credulity to a
fare-thee-well. You gave her to think that you believed her
story of coming upon an already mortally wounded Whelan
and then giving him the *coup de grâce* pursuant to some pact
they had putatively entered into. Anyone who would believe
that would believe that she just took the pistol home and
buried it in her garden."

"Close. It's in a large planter on her patio."

"Go get it."

"You mean, dig it up and take it away?"

"Yes."

"Without telling her?"

"Why should you?"

"But that would be stealing."

"Would you rather I went and did it for you?"

How like a mother she was when she wanted to get her
way. Or a nagging wife. A man will take much from a
woman under the general if tacit promise of sexual rewards

in the future, but this was a weapon unavailable to Gwen. It would be crude to say her power over me lay in her money. She had other assets as well, among them organizational skills, the company clerk virtues I have mentioned many times. They are real. They are motive enough. Besides I wanted to get away from her withering contemptuous glare.

"What will you do when I am gone?"

"Rochester's visit suggests that I should take another and closer look into the lugubrious Corcoran."

"Just so you have something to do while I am gone."

The sound of a jumbo paperback edition of *War and Peace* hitting a just closed door can be taken as the audible symbol of my odd partnership with Gwen Probst. Will you think less of me if I mention that I set out for my hitherto unplanned morning after the night-before visit to B. O. Wolfe with a zestful springy step of which I was ashamed even at the time? I put myself in mind of Chaucer's chanticleer. Is this the purpose of life, to strut rooster-like from one effort at fecundation to another? Have I been reduced to my loins? Who is master here, the organ or the organist? My foot was heavy on the pedal as I drove.

9

To Carthage then I came, as Austin put it, with etc., etc. But the great Bishop of Hippo was looking back on youthful indiscretion while I at my age was still mired in a veritable potomos of passion. With no sense whatsoever of walking through water, I hurried to the door and leaned into the bell.

A half-minute passed. I rang again. Minutes of ringing and no response and my heated imagination tormented me with images of the night before. And of the moment. How could I not imagine her crouched within, keeping quiet, hoping I would go away? The morning light had brought her to her senses. The thought of having done such things with the likes of me filled her with self-loathing. My arrival conveniently transferred the loathing to me.

The door was never answered. I shifted weight from foot to foot, scanned the sky, I tried insouciant whistling. Finally like a whipped cur I crept down to my car. After several attempts, I got it started and went with much wheezing and rattling up the street. The motor died half a block away and I directed my no longer automotive vehicle to the curb. I put my forehead against the hands that gripped the wheel and felt an urge to cry.

Thus it was that I had unwittingly concealed myself from the car that soon roared past, coming from the building in which B.O. lived. The aggravating sound of a car doing what a car should do caused me to lift my head just as the car went past. At its wheel, oblivious to everything but the road ahead, was George Corcoran.

Who has fathomed the workings of the human mind? Not Locke, not Hume, not Dr. Ruth. My own mind frequently induces awe in me. In a trice I was out of my car and sprinting back to B.O.'s. I did not bother with the door but went around the building toward the river. I realized that the night before when we were out on her patio burying the pistol, I had unconsciously thought of ways in which a thief or other intruder could gain access to B.O.'s river front dwelling. Minutes later, I was tying up a stolen skiff below her patio and clambering onto it. The first thing I noticed was the mess someone had made of the planter. It looked as if some animal had been digging in it, perhaps a rat terrier, scattering dirt every which way. I hurried to it. This was not the work of a dog digging up a bone. The pistol was missing.

I turned to the sliding doors leading from the patio into the living room. They were not completely closed. I went to them, put out my hand, then stopped. The scene suggested caution. That I sensed this even before I noticed the body lying on the floor of the living room goes a long way toward establishing that intuition is not an exclusively feminine thing. Or that no one is devoid of some feminine traits. Or neither. In any case, there was no mistaking the fact that it was B. O. Wolfe who lay on her own floor, on her back, staring unblinkingly at the ceiling. Whence came the certitude that this was not an exotic form of eastern meditation? Perhaps from the traces of blood at her nostrils and at the floorward corner of her mouth. Was this the body which a few short hours ago . . . But I stopped such philosophizing. I felt a powerful urge to get out of there.

I went the way I had come, not returning the purloined boat to its proper place, but rowing away from it, beaching it and then scrambling toward the nearest pay phone from which I could call Gwen.

"Dead?"

"As in lifeless. And I have a good idea who did it."

"How good?"

"Leaving the scene of the crime just minutes before I found the body, previously having rung the bell without effect, was none other than George Corcoran. Come pick me up. My car died too."

"But I am due to meet George Corcoran in ten minutes."

"Don't you dare."

"Ish, if what you say is true, well . . ."

I broke in. "If what I say is true you'd be a damned fool to be alone with that man."

"People used to tell me that about you."

"I've never been alone with George Corcoran."

"Take a taxi. Come to Corcoran's office if you want. I'm keeping that appointment."

I took a bus. For one thing, I was out of change and couldn't make another call. For another, the bus swung into the curb as I was standing there, and onto it I jumped.

"All I have is a dollar," I told the driver.

"The fare is two dollars."

"You're kidding."

"Of course. I have a pathological desire to tell jokes. I mean I can't make change. You don't have a buck and a quarter we round it off to the nearest bill."

"I think I'll go into the bus business."

"Don't."

Whatever the driver's pathological desires, driving in a straight line was not one of them. He maneuvered his vehicle through nonexistent traffic, perhaps practicing for the rush hour, and it swayed like a circus ride as I made my way down the aisle. The plastic-scooped seat received me with something of the readiness of the leather chairs in B.O.'s television room. B.O. That horny woman, so full of life, was dead. She may not have had a pact with Corcoran, but he had sped her into the bourne from which no traveler returns. Thanking God for my padded bum, I bounced along, putting it all together. Having done in Michael Whelan, Corcoran the orthodontist—are there any heterodontists?—had then done away with the late entrepreneur's paramour. Perhaps she had seen him at the scene of the crime or, just as bad, he thought she had seen him. Why? Because he had seen her. No sooner had his fell deed been done than she came on the scene. He watched in puzzled horror when she shot his victim.

The pistol had been dug up from the grave B.O. and I had placed it in last night. Corcoran was now in possession of that gun. I cursed myself for putting it into a baggie before we buried it. It would be in working order. And Gwen Probst, against my express order, was even now (checking my watch) meeting with George Corcoran. The bus had arrived downtown. The great bulk of the courthouse rose before me. Not far away I would find police headquarters. It seemed time to put Brunswick into the picture.

Brunswick had been an instructor in the police academy when I went through. At the time I thought I had a vocation to the constabulary, but the boredom of duty gave me time to read and I was bitten definitively by the PI bug. I apprenticed under a shady character, since gone to God, and it was there that I met Gwen Probst. Brunswick and I had crossed swords over the years—he moonlighted as a fencing instructor and I took lessons from time to time—but there was a linking kind of mutual dislike that bound us together.

"Get out of here," Brunswick said when I looked into his office.

"Wait till I get in."

"Do you know that joke?"

Brunswick has an oblique and earthy sense of humor. At any other time, I might have humored him. Now I was all business.

"I have solved the Michael Whelan murder."

"Murder? You're crazy. He fell and hit his head."

"Sparky Sequin found a bullet in him."

"It's not in his report."

"Probably because it wasn't the cause of death."

"Look, Slattery, you and I could pick up a bullet driving through town at any time of the day or night. Read the paper. Whelan fell and hit his head and don't encourage his widow to think otherwise."

"Does the name B. O. Wolfe mean anything to you?"

"No."

Of course not. But this was not the time to lecture Brunswick about how sloppy he had become. Just because there are lots of murders doesn't mean that some of them shouldn't be properly investigated. Brunswick should have found that list of customers, he should have checked out the people on it. If he had, B. O. Wolfe might be alive today. On the other hand, I might not have spent last night with her.

"Whelan sold her a course. They were having an affair. She is now lying dead on the floor of the living room at this address." I tossed a slip of paper onto the desk. "George Corcoran was seen leaving the scene of the crime, minutes before the body was discovered."

"By whom."

"Never mind by whom."

"Youm?"

"George Corcoran is armed and desperate. My associate Gwen Probst is with him now, diverting him until we arrive."

"Is she still pulling your chestnuts out of the fire?"

"I won't dignify that with an answer."

"I always liked that girl. She would make a good cop."

Brunswick pushed back from his desk.

"Where are they?"

"I'll show you."

He stopped on the way to the door, then shrugged. "I guess you better come along at that."

10

Taciturnity, Gwen has told me, is highly recommended in the twelve-runged ladder leading to humility. My taciturnity on the way to Corcoran's office was unrelated to humility, its acquisition or loss. In any case, humility is not a virtue appropriate to my state in life. What I was enjoying was the silent satisfaction of having done a tough job well. Mrs. Whelan would cash in on what I had done. Whatever monetary compensation might come my way was as nothing to the pleasure in a job well done.

Nor will I conceal from my friendly reader that I took a more suspicious pleasure in having bested Gwen. It would be absurd to call our relation competitive. For all her merits, and they are few, *pace* Inspector Brunswick, Gwen simply did not have the mind for investigative work. She did however pay my rent and run those silly ads and drive me around in her Cherokee. Would I do the same for her if I won the lottery? Such hypothetical questions can be useful in the revelation of character. Before we had arrived I had resolved to share my triumph with Gwen—not fifty/fifty, more like twenty/eighty, some pretense that without her I would not have cornered George Corcoran.

"Remember, Brunswick. He's armed."

"So was the Venus de Milo."

But I saw him pat the appropriate part of his anatomy as we started for the clinic door. He was armed.

I got to the door first, and brought a finger to my lips. I put my ear to the door. A moment later, I was stumbling into the hall. Brunswick had pushed open the door. Now he stepped over me, and called out, "Dr. Corcoran?"

"In here."

The voice was that of Gwen. A door opened and she was framed in it. She glanced at Brunswick, then smiled at me.

"I thought you'd bring him."

"Is Corcoran here?"

"I've done everything you said, Ish. Come in, Inspector. You will find that Ishmael Slattery has made your trip worthwhile."

The office was that of Rochester, not Corcoran, but both partners were there, as was Rose. She was no longer radiant and cuddly but withdrawn and morose, out of her manic phase. Gwen led me to the desk and pulled out the high-backed chair for me. I sat and looked at the three people whose lives would be forever altered by what transpired now. Gwen found a folding chair for Brunswick, and settled him in a corner. Not punishment. It put him between the three others and the door.

"All right, Corcoran," I began. "Where's the pistol?"

"Why don't I start at the beginning?" Gwen came and stood at my side. "Mr. Slattery is apt to give you too lean a version of what he has accomplished. I suffer from no such compunction. I am perfectly willing to praise him to the skies."

A groan arose from Brunswick in his folding chair.

"Inspector Brunswick, from whom you have just heard, is here to make the arrest. One of you, of course, murdered Michael Whelan."

Corcoran yawned, Rochester lit a cigarette and Rose threw back her head and emitted a soulful wail.

"Rose presented an interesting possibility, of course. She had motive and presumably opportunity. In some cycles of her personality, she is capable of remarkable physical feats."

"She can hit a ball over two hundred yards," Rochester said, getting interested. "A golf ball," he added, turning to Brunswick.

"Mr. Slattery dismissed the possibility, however, and of course he was right."

"Absolutely." Rochester glared at his son-in-law and eased his chair back next to Brunswick's.

I sat forward, anxious to tell how I had settled on George Corcoran. Gwen put a hand on my arm and I sat back. After all, it was pleasant to hear her account of what I had done.

106

"Understandably, perhaps, I then thought that it must be George Corcoran, and Mr. Slattery fed this suspicion when he saw Corcoran scampering away from the apartment in which B. O. Wolfe, another Whelan client, and one with whom he had conducted a sordid affair, even as I speak lies dead. Surely, I thought, that clinches it."

She turned and her smile seemed to beg my indulgence for her silly thoughts about George Corcoran. But I was loath to interrupt.

"Strengthening this suspicion was the fact that George Corcoran too had been having an affair with B. O. Wolfe, apparently a woman of insatiable sensuous appetite."

"No," cried Rochester, leaping to his feet and covering his daughter's ears. "Rose mustn't hear these things."

"There you have it," Gwen said, advancing toward Rochester. "That was your motive all along, wasn't it? To protect your daughter."

"I don't know what you're talking about," Rochester said, regaining his seat next to Brunswick.

Corcoran rose and smacked his forehead with an open hand. "Then why did you tell me Rose killed Whelan and then, having learned about Beryl, shot her? He sent me there to retrieve the pistol from where he said she had buried it."

Corcoran stood and went to his wife, taking her in his arms. She pressed mewling against him. It was a tender moment. Rochester rose but Brunswick took hold of his arm and reseated him forcibly.

"Why did you kill Whelan?" Brunswick demanded of the senior partner.

"That," said Gwen, "is the most fascinating thing of all. May I finish, Ish?"

I made a weary gesture and settled back, enjoying my moment of triumph.

"Further interviews with Scott Terrill, the manager of the former hotel in which Michael Whelan had his offices, revealed that Dr. Rochester had been an adamant opponent of the sect's purchase of the building. He would not buy it himself, but he was against their buying it. You and I would suppose that religious prejudice underlay his attitude." Her hand was once again on my arm. Her hands are her best feature. Elongated, with thin and graceful fingers, nails done to a turn, just a clear polish. No rings. "Ishmael Slattery was unsatisfied with so banal an explanation. It is his belief that the want of true religious prejudice is a sign of the blandness of the present age. No, there had to be some other reason why Dr. Rochester felt so strongly about that hotel."

Rochester had risen to his feet, his expression now one of unutterable desolation. Brunswick did not prevent his rising. "Hilda and I, years ago, Hilda . . ." And then he broke down. Brunswick eased him into his chair.

"You can see now why Mr. Slattery feels no sense of triumph. Dr. Corcoran and his wife honeymooned in that hotel. That it should become anything other than what it had once been was intolerable to him. He felt that his life was becoming unmoored. His wife passed on, his son-in-law, devoted as he was to Rose, nonetheless had succumbed to the blandishments of B.O. Wolfe. When he learned that a charlatan like Michael Whalen actually occupied the sainted bridal suite as his office, something snapped in a formerly noble mind. Inspector, Dr. Rochester is yours." Gwen turned to me. "It is a privilege to work with you."

11

Odds and ends, it has been said, are the essentials of history. Don't ask me who said it. My memory is beginning to go.

There are things I myself have said and done that I no longer remember. Gwen, bless her shapeless body, functions as a memory for me.

"An external drive?"

"I don't understand."

"That is because you are computer illiterate."

"For the which, may God be praised."

"I hope you don't mean that witch, B. O. Wolfe."

It was Gwen's great regret that Beryl Olive Wolfe had not turned out to be Michael Whelan's killer. She could have taken satisfaction in seeing such a rutting beast (her phrase) brought to heel.

"She wasn't exactly innocent."

"That's what I mean. She was a one-woman sexual revolution. Shameless."

It seemed best to say nothing. The sinner feels an odd comradeship with his fellows. It is difficult to strike a righteous stance—difficult, not impossible.

"I meant the bullet."

"You heard Rochester."

The orthodontist, eager to confess, had told all. B.O. had indeed come upon the murder scene at an awkward moment and she had taken a shot. She was aiming at Rochester. She missed and hit the fallen body of Michael Whelan. He wrested the gun from her and eventually used it to silence her. The gun B.O. and I had buried in the planter? Police tests showed that it was not the weapon used either on Whalen or on B.O. herself.

I borrowed Gwen's Cherokee, telling her I needed to be by myself. I drove to B.O.'s apartment and let myself in with the key I had borrowed from Brunswick. From the living room, I looked out onto the patio. A squirrel was in the planter, digging away, spraying dirt everywhere. He scampered away when I came out. Five minutes later, I found the baggie, where B.O. and I had buried it. I looked at it for a time, a wry smile on my face, then leaned over the railing and dropped it into the river. Captain Ahab would have persisted, but look what happened to him. If you don't remember, call me. Ishmael.

THE SINCEREST FORM OF SLATTERY

1

"May I call you Ishmael?"

Her hair was long and straight, sun-bleached rather than natural blond, and her face with its high molded cheeks was done to a turn. Her sea blue eyes looked me right in the eyes but her tanned flesh was as out of place in this climate as the outfit she wore. She had opened her coat, as if hearing a drumbeat or a snarling sax, squirmed out of it and then let it fall back over the chair I pointed her to. Underneath was beachwear, a striped purple and white billowy blouse that tied low on her slim hips, and what used to be called pedal pushers. She was freckled as well as deeply tanned. Obviously a dame who didn't know enough to come in out of the sun but she had walked out of a snowstorm into my office and asked if she could call me Ishmael.

"Not on the first date."

Her smile revealed long strong teeth. Even at my age, my first thought was how we might run away and live in sin together. Her smile faded and it was as if the thermostat had been lowered.

"Someone is trying to kill me."

"Would you like some coffee?"

She was shocked. "Do you know what coffee does to you?"

"It keeps me warm and awake. And it goes well with cigarettes."

"You smoke too?"

"Only when lit." I took out a crushed pack of Luckies, then put them away. They're a prop. I had quit. Just that morning. I couldn't stop coughing while I shaved and my wounded face looked like it. But what could I lose? This doll had obviously come to the wrong office and after some harmless badinage would realize her mistake and go.

"Why did you come to me?"

"I just flew in from Sarasota."

"I wondered about the fur coat."

She was maybe in her early twenties but looked like a college freshman—to be taken inclusively—when she smiled.

"It's imitation. Even so, I feel bad wearing it."

"You'd freeze without it."

"I can't stand the thought of killing animals for their skin."

"That's why I go barefoot."

She suppressed her smile and shook her head. "You're as bad as he said."

"Who recommended me?"

"Oh it wasn't a recommendation. I sat next to a policeman on the plane and asked him about private investigators."

At least it hadn't been just another dissatisfied client. "What was his name?"

"Brunswick."

"He's an old friend." I took out the Luckies, then put them away again.

"He sounded more like an enemy," she said.

"It's his manner. An affectation. He envies me."

"He said you were the worst private investigator he knows."

"So you decided to come to me."

"Can I be honest?"

Not an auspicious beginning, but I have learned to take the cards I am dealt. When you have the name Ishmael Slattery you had better be good or, if not good, philosophical. In any case, I was doing what I liked, it was better than working and, when things got very rough, I could fall back on Gwen Probst. Not literally. Although even literally she would at least try to break my fall. I had been very aware of Gwen's presence in the next office ever since the blonde walked in. Put them side by side and it wouldn't be Before and After. More like Now and Never.

The blonde's name was Dagmar West. Of course that was her professional name.

"Like yours."

"Mine's real."

"Come on. Ishy-male?"

"Ishmael. Two and a half syllables. What's your real name?"

"Mary Milosovich."

She had grown up in Chicago, attended the parish school, Transfiguration, then a public high school which had been preparation for life in the real world. She had come to think of school as combat training. No wonder she left as quickly as she could. To model. I waited. We live in a world of euphemisms.

"Model as in escort?"

Her teeth closed on her lower lip and she nodded. I got up and closed the door to Gwen's office, refilled my cup, got settled. "Tell me about it."

Her story was a familiar one, but however trite, it happens only once to each victim and the fact that it has happened to others would not cushion the blow.

"He said with my looks I should be on television. And I believed him."

He would start her small, he said, as one of the girls on quiz shows who carried cards around or turned over letters, then she would go on to be the sidekick of someone like Regis Philbin. After that, who knows? In the meantime, just to get used to an audience, he had booked her into this club as a dancer.

"A stripper."

She heaved a sigh. Even in a smoky, boozy, ill-lit dive, she would be something to look at. I asked her about the smoke.

"I wore a mask."

"Sure."

"I was sort of the cat woman and wore a cat's head. So I bought one of those masks painters wear."

"What was your manager's name?"

"Joe Derringer."

"Local?"

"More like an express."

"You didn't get that tan in a smoky club."

"He also has tanning parlors."

"Ah."

Between dancing weeks, Derringer had put her to work in the Spumento Spa. "I wore a black wig and said I was Japanese. My specialty was walking barefoot on people's backs."

When Derringer flew her to Florida, there was no longer any equivocation about her job.

"It took a while, but finally I figured it out. Am I dumb? Up until a week ago, I still thought all this was leading to a television career."

A throat cleared in the next room, very close. Gwen must be crouched by the door, listening. Unnecessary, really, since she bugged my office in order to record just such occasions as this, infrequent as, alas, they were.

"You said your life is being threatened."

"He said he would kill me if I ever tried to quit."

"Nonsense. This is America. We've only lost one war. Lincoln freed the slaves."

"You from the South?"

"Do I look Vietnamese?"

"Joe said Lincoln only freed the blacks."

"No Japanese?"

"He meant it."

"You want protection, is that it?" I sat upright, eased my shoulders back, gave her a glimpse of my chest expansion.

"I want to get out of town."

"This isn't a travel office."

"I need a new identification."

"Why did you come back here from Florida?"

My question puzzled her. "Chicago's my home town."

"You just got back and you want to leave?"

"What makes you think I just got back?"

"Your clothes?"

"I like to be comfortable."

"What do you want?"

"I want to stop being me."

The break in the lighting beneath her door indicated that Gwen wasn't missing a word of this. She wanted it live as well as a taped rerun. I pressed her buzzer and could hear her leap in surprise. The door opened almost immediately.

"Did you get all that?"

Gwen surveyed the considerable proportions of Dagmar West, no doubt thinking it would be difficult to disguise such endowments.

"What's the problem?"

I gave her a short version, knowing she had heard the long.

"No problem," Gwen said, as if we did a brisk business in wetbacks. "Dye the hair, change your name, get you appropriate ID, maybe stash you in a convent for a while."

"A convent!"

"You won't have to take vows."

"After where I've been, you want me to live in a convent?"

I suggested to Gwen that she come up with something better. And I wanted anything and everything she could dig up on Joe Derringer.

"It's already on your computer."

So she had been doing more than eavesdropping since Dagmar arrived. Gwen had pulled up from a database a dossier on Derringer. I perused it while the two ladies set off to the ladies'.

"Can I leave this here?" Dagmar asked.

It was a blue canvas sports bag she had carried slung over the imitation fur covering her shoulder.

"Sure."

She tossed it to me. I stood to catch it and was driven back to the wall.

"What's in it?" I eased it to the floor.

"Costumes," she said prettily. "And things."

I felt the perverse tremor felt by members of the British cabinet at the thought of lingerie.

Half an hour later, they had not returned, so I went down the hall to knock on the door. But the door of the powder room was open.

"Gwen!"

My voice echoed through the suite. Dark thoughts ran through my mind. A jealous Gwen had taken Dagmar out and dropped her off the bridge into the Chicago River. With her bosom, she would float. The ringing phone took me back to my desk.

"We got both of them."

"The left and the right?"

"The blonde and your office boy."

"That's no office boy. That's a dame."

"She fought like a man. Go to the public phone on the corner and wait."

The phone slammed in my ear. From the window I looked out at snow falling on Chicago. What kind of villain was he anyway, choosing an outdoor booth in this kind of weather? I sensed I was up against a ruthless adversary. How painful it was to think of Mary Milosovich, aka Dagmar West, kidnapped. And Gwen too, sort of.

2

I brought my car around and parked within hearing range of the outside phone and, using my car phone, called Brunswick.

"The Inspector is busy. Would you care to leave a message?"

"Tell him I represent the blonde from Sarasota."

"How do you spell that?"

"B-l-o-n . . ."

Brunswick came on, his tone testy. "Is that you, Slattery?"

"Thanks for the referral."

"What's this about Sarasota?"

"Did you come right from Midway to the office?"

"I've been back a week. That blonde really come to see you?"

"Just today."

"I'm surprised she came at all after what I told her."

"Why *did* you tell her about me?"

"As a warning."

"Well, now she's missing."

"She shouldn't be hard to find."

"They snatched Gwen too."

"Well, that rules out White Slavery. How long ago was this?"

I looked at my watch. I shook it. The battery must be dead. "Minutes ago. I am parked by an outdoor phone awaiting further instructions."

"Well, keep me posted."

He actually hung up. I angrily punched redial but just then the pay phone began to ring. On the sidewalk, pedestrians paused and looked at it, then looked at one another. I clambered out of the car and grabbed the instrument just before another hand closed over mine.

"It's for me," I explained.

His was an evil grin. The teeth he still had would soon go the way of those he had lost. "How can you tell?"

"Count the rings."

While he considered that, I said into the phone, "Slattery."

"Have you called the cops?" It was the same voice.

"Are you crazy?"

"I want you to call the cops. I want you to tell them everything. Got that?"

"What about the girls?"

Once more the phone was unceremoniously slammed in my ear. The tooth-impaired man had been loitering while I talked, and now came up to me.

"Are you Slattery?"

"Why do you ask?"

"Derringer wants to see you."

His mouth was closed but one incisor insisted on taking the air. His bloodshot eyes had the unfocused look of one who has kept reality at bay for most of his life. Was it plausible that Joe Derringer would use this derelict as his messenger? But if this man was from Derringer, who was that on the phone? The derelict was tugging at my sleeve.

"Just a minute. I've got to make a call."

That's when I realized he was carrying a knife. He put the tip of it shakily against my midsection. The fact that he looked new to surgery made him more menacing rather than less.

"Now."

"That's my car."

"We're walking."

"I can't just leave it there."

"We'll take care of it."

"You touch that car and . . ."

I could feel the tip of the blade through my waistcoat. He made a head feint, indicating that I should start walking. I did. I swung down the middle of the walk with my derelict escort puffing to keep up with me. I swung my arms like a British subaltern and tried to engage the eyes of those I passed. That was easy enough, but conveying to them that I was being taken somewhere against my will was harder. Gwen had been nagging me about getting out of this neighborhood but where was I going to get offices like mine for four hundred a month?

"You pay four hundred a month for this?" Gwen had said, looking around with curled lip. She is independently wealthy, through no fault of her own, but works with me because she has designs on my body. No, that isn't fair. Gwen thinks in terms of permanence. It told against her that she would want to marry me but it also tells you why I am unlikely to acquiesce.

Just when I had decided that Gwen was right about the lack of solidarity among my neighbors, I saw the patrol car on the opposite side of the street. I turned to see if my toothless escort had seen it. He was nowhere in sight. I craned my neck to look over the pedestrians, but there was no sign of the derelict.

I am still a young man, but there are times when my memory tricks me. Have you ever arrived at work and been unable to recall the drive that brought you there? Have you ever found yourself unable to remember whose deal it is? I found myself wondering if I had imagined that hand closing on mine when I picked up the outside phone. But I knew I could not have imagined his jack o'lantern grin.

The patrol car executed a screeching U-turn, its siren growling, but this did not stop drivers from making honking comments on the maneuver. Brunswick hopped out and Gwen was with him.

"They let me go," she said, clutching at my arm. "They dropped me off at the precinct."

"Derringer wants you to know he kidnapped Dagmar," I told Brunswick.

The inspector wore a tweed jacket, a denim shirt and a western tie. He was telling the cops to make the pedestrians move along. The patrol car had climbed the curb before coming to a stop and was undeniably something to excite curiosity. Gwen was babbling to me of her ordeal. Thank God the kidnappers had not realized they had an heiress as well as Dagmar in their clutches. But would they have chosen differently if they had known? My eye crept up the street.

"My car's missing," I cried.

"You called me to report a missing car?"

"I called you from the car. It was parked there, by that phone booth."

"Maybe it was ticketed and towed."

I knew better. In my mind's eye I saw the toothless derelict at the wheel of my car, going pell-mell God knows where. To Derringer? But he had said Derringer wanted to see me, he had pressed a knife against my tum-tum.

"You need a good cup of tea," I said solicitously to Gwen. "Will you excuse us, Inspector?"

"What kind of tea?"

"Oolong. You wouldn't like it."

"It's been too long since I've had some."

He dismissed the patrol car and the three of us went back up the sidewalk toward my building. We were twenty yards from it when the explosion rocked the street.

It was ahead of us. I began to run. But thinking better of it I stopped, turned and started back toward the explosion, hurrying to catch up with Gwen. Brunswick, rooted to the sidewalk, watched me go by.

"My office," I shouted.

Smoke was rolling from a pair of windows on the fourth floor. It was my office. Gwen darted into the building. When I came in, the lights above the elevator indicated it was on the rise. I entered the stairway and began to take them two at a time all the way to 2. I settled for a step at a time from 2 to 3. I slowed to a walk. On the landing between 3 and 4, I stopped, huffing and puffing, my heart pounding in my rib cage. I pulled myself up the final flight and stumbled into the smoke-filled hallway.

"Gwen," I called. "Gwen."

What had been the door of my office had been blown across the hall, sucking furniture after it. Papers were everywhere. I stood and looked into the haze. Gwen appeared, coming toward me.

"My office is all right. Yours isn't."

"Dagmar's sports bag," I said.

I stared into the smoke. Below in the street, there was the sound of fire engines. My office was torn all to hell.

"I have all the records backed up," Gwen said reassuringly. "There wasn't anything valuable in here."

"Not with me gone."

She put a hand on my arm and squeezed. I felt the intimation of a surge of equivocal affection for my partner.

Brunswick arrived, and then the firemen, lustily laying about them with axes. Gwen stood in the doorway of her office, arms outspread, and dared them to enter. When the inviolability of her workspace was established, she joined Brunswick and me.

"This might be a good time to retire," Brunswick said, lighting a cigar.

"This is a No Smoking zone," I said, my eyes smarting from the cloud still rolling from my office. From inside came the sound of ripping and tearing as public servants saved my property by destroying it.

"Let's get out of here," Gwen suggested.

"Not until I find out what happened."

Gwen took one of my arms and Brunswick the other and I was led away to the elevator.

In a nearby saloon, over corned beef and cabbage and a shared pitcher of beer, we reviewed the day.

Out of the cold had come Mary Milosovich, clad in summer clothes and an imitation fur, claiming her life was in danger. She had heard of me from Brunswick.

"That was a week ago," Brunswick said, puffing on his cigar while Gwen fanned away the smoke with a menu.

"A flight from Florida."

"Is that what she said?"

"Isn't that how it happened?"

"What would I be doing in Florida this time of year?"

"Getting warm?"

"She's talking about Sarasota, Minnesota. That's the last place she worked for Derringer."

"She told you about Derringer?"

"It helped pass the time."

"On the plane?"

"On the CTA from O'Hare. I had put my wife on a plane and was returning to the city. She sat next to me."

"What was she wearing?"

The garb he described was the garb she had been wearing when she came to my office.

"A week ago?"

Brunswick nodded. "How's the corned beef?"

"What's she been doing for a week?"

"Probably dancing in Derringer's dive in Old Town."

"Did she say she was going there?"

"She said she was going to kill herself."

Gwen sat back, horrified. "What did you tell her?"

"That's when I thought of you, Slattery. This dame didn't know what down was. I figured talking to you would cheer her up."

"Her sports bag must have been full of explosives," Gwen said.

"But why?"

"Don't assume she meant to leave it there. Remember we were kidnapped."

Brunswick asked to hear about that.

"She went in first and I waited. When it was my turn I heard a scuffle outside. By the time I got the door open, they were dragging her into the stairwell. I went after them."

"Them?"

One of her assailants sounded like the derelict with the

jack o'lantern smile with whom I had dealt at the outdoor phone booth.

"He said Derringer wanted to see me," I said. "He pulled a knife. I walked half a block before I realized he wasn't behind me."

Brunswick found this amusing. His laughter shook the ash from his cigar and it dropped to the tabletop, retaining the shape of the bit of cigar, a corpse whose soul has fled.

"Was the toothless man working for or against Derringer?" Gwen asked.

"Ditto for Dagmar," I said.

Brunswick pushed back from the table. "Close your office, go to Florida, sit in the sun."

"After someone blew up my office?"

"Gwen may be right. It was probably an accident."

He left without paying for his share of the beer. Gwen brushed the cigar ash from the table.

"He's right, Ish. We should get out of here, take a trip . . ."

Whatever attraction such a cowardly exit might have was dimmed by the thought of Gwen in a bikini, her stick figure casting a minimum shadow on the Florida sands.

"I'm going to see Derringer."

She gripped my arm. "No."

I patted her hand then pried it loose from my arm, a grim determined look on my face. Derringer's place in Old Town boasted 24-Hour Nudes. It had been months since I had been there.

3

The music was taped, the volume an assault on the ear; the ill-lit place pulsed with its savage rhythm. On the stage behind the bar a girl wearing pasties and the figment of a sequined fig leaf writhed as if in passion to the music's beat. The lights trained on her were solid with serpentine smoke. I went among the largely abandoned tables toward the silhouetted customers at the bar. The bartender was half-turned toward the dancer, watching her antics with jaded disinterest.

The music crescendoed, the dancer went into a frenzy of simulated passion involving a pole which she also used to pivot herself offstage when finally the music gave way to a silence punctuated with feeble applause from the men at the bar. I took a stool and assumed the expression of a gawking tourist.

"Hi, Slattery," the bartender said.

"I don't know you."

"Derringer wants to see you."

"Yeah?"

Abruptly music began again, as loud as before. Another wench was on the runway, apparently in heat. A man with a face that would have given Darwin joy stood beside me. He took me firmly by the arm, eased me off my stool and propelled me at an undignified pace through the murky atmosphere to an office in the rear. I was pushed inside. When the door closed behind me I realized I was in the john. Only there weren't any urinals. The sound of flushing from one of the stalls filled me with panic. I turned and grabbed the door but it was locked.

"Thanks for coming, Ishy-male."

I turned to face Dagmar West, emerging from the stall. She shut the door behind her. It was impossible to think of her as Mary Milosovich in the outfit she wore.

"I can usually be found in the ladies' room," I said.

"No one will ever suspect we're meeting here."

"Derringer wants to see me."

125

"The bartender told you that."

I nodded. She nodded.

"That's what he was supposed to say."

"Isn't it true?"

She hesitated, then stepped aside and opened the stall door. A man with a glassy stare sat on the stool, slumped sideways so that his shoulder leaned against the wall. I turned my eyes to Dagmar.

"Meet the late Joe Derringer."

"What happened?"

"He's been shot."

"In the ladies' room?"

"It was where we met."

"Who did it?"

She opened her purse and took a gun from it, holding it by the barrel. She handed it to me.

"I found this beside the body."

"When?"

"Just before I went to see you."

"You left a gym bag in my office."

"I'll pick it up later."

"It had a bomb in it."

In the circumstances her throaty laughter seemed in bad taste. I told her about the shambles my office was in. A frown formed on her face. A knock on the door transformed her. She began to scream and to back away from me. The pounding on the door became louder. I looked at the door and then at the screaming Dagmar. The sound of smashing wood and fittings becoming unmoored told me we had visitors. Brunswick stepped into the room. He stopped abruptly and raised his arms. I realized I was still holding the gun Dagmar had handed me.

"Put that down, you idiot."

But the weapon gave me a sense of power. Disrespectful as Brunswick's tone was, I could see the fear in his eyes.

Dagmar slithered past me, still whimpering, and sought refuge with Brunswick. Through the shattered door the bartender and several of the ecdysiasts were visible. Brunswick removed his jacket and was about to drape it over Dagmar's frail shoulders when suddenly he threw it at me. He came right along with it and I was driven across the room. When I hit the stall door, it popped open. Brunswick pulled me out of the way and stared at Derringer.

"Is he finished?"

"Well, I heard the sound of flushing when I came in."

"He's dead," Dagmar wailed. "And he did it."

She was pointing at me. I looked down at the gun I held. I began to hand it to Brunswick but he caught me with a chopping movement of his hand and I sank boneless to the tile floor.

My situation was patiently explained to me by Brunswick in an interrogation room downtown. I was a hired assassin in the pay of those who wished to wrest control of Derringer's skin joints from him. He was betting that the gun he had taken from me in the women's room of the Ooo la la was the weapon that had killed Derringer. My prints were all over it. Dagmar had pretended to be my accomplice but would now do whatever was required to make me pay my debt to society.

"Do you believe that?" I did not sound as incredulous as I sought to.

He looked impassively at me. "It's dumb enough to be true."

"Brunswick, I am not that dumb. You sent that girl to me. She left a bomb in my office."

"Why would she want to kill you?"

"Have you asked her that?"

Brunswick laid his hands flat on the table between us. "She said she doesn't know anything about a bomb."

"You saw my office."

"She thinks it was meant for her."

"For her!"

I explained to Brunswick that Dagmar had asked to leave her bag in my office.

"When she tossed it to me, I nearly dropped it, it was so heavy."

"Dynamite isn't heavy."

"Is that what it was?"

"Pieces of what may have been a timing device were found."

"There!"

"You wouldn't be the first mad bomber who was his own victim."

"I was with you in the street."

"You were smart enough to get out of there before it blew."

I had the feeling he was toying with me. We were old enemies, to be sure. Once he had been my superior, but I had left the force to become a freelance defender of justice, the kind most despised by my former colleagues, a private eye. Brunswick and I had crossed swords both before and after my declaration of independence. He was a bastard but he was fair.

He left me alone in the empty interrogation room, but the place seemed full of unanswered questions. I tried not to think, assuming I was being observed through one-way glass. At the mirror, I straightened my tie, then winked and minced across the room.

"What's wrong with you?" Brunswick said, coming in.

"Sciatica."

"Maybe you can get a job in one of Derringer's joints after you've served your sentence."

"Brunswick, I did not bomb my own office. I did not shoot Derringer."

"Well, you didn't shoot Derringer anyway."

The bullets in the body had not come from the gun Dagmar had foisted on me. I was free.

"What brought you to the Ooo la la by the way?" I asked Brunswick.

"A routine raid."

"Ha. You, raiding skin joints?"

"I got a call."

"Saying what?"

He rubbed beneath his chin as if to firm it up. "It was Derringer. He said his life was being threatened. He also said he had some new girls and I was welcome as his guest."

"He sounded worried?"

"Well you know how unreliable new girls can be."

"I was set up, Brunswick."

"Why you?"

"That's what I intend to find out."

When he checked me out, Gwen was waiting for me. And Dagmar. The dancer had her false fur draped over her shoulders and beneath it she wore the kind of simple dress my sister might have worn. Or Gwen. She looked at me warily.

"Did he confess?" she asked Brunswick.

"I'm waiting for absolution."

"You shouldn't joke about things like that."

"You shouldn't tell lies about me."

Her face took on a sad expression, directed at Brunswick.

"It all started when you recommended Mr. Slattery to me."

"You call that a recommendation?"

"What do you call it?"

"Fair warning."

Dagmar turned to me. "Can we talk?"

"We seem to be."

"I mean just us."

Gwen squared her shoulders and came between us. "I wish we'd stashed you in a convent."

The idea didn't seem as improbable now, Dagmar being dressed as she was. The simple frock made few concessions to the natural undulations of her body. She was almost as shapeless as Gwen. Her face was free of makeup and the reddish hair that had been covered with a wig was cropped closer to her head. I learned that, like me, she had been in custody.

"What for?"

"Material witness. I told them I had seen you shoot Derringer."

"Thanks."

"It was every man for himself."

In order to speak to me, she kept moving her head, trying to avoid the intervening Gwen.

I reasonably asked, "If neither of us shot him, who did?"

"Where can we be alone?"

Gwen's right lifted and caught Dagmar under the chin. The ecdysiast lifted with the uppercut, her eyes glazed and she sank to the floor. I scooted around Gwen and tried to get my arms under Dagmar's but my aim was off. Gwen's wasn't. She caught me on the side of the jaw. My last memory was of sinking into the plush bounty of Dagmar.

4

I awoke in my own bed. I don't know how I got home. Gwen sat beside the bed, her expression one of rueful concern.

"I'm sorry I hit you."

I said nothing. How could I acknowledge that a woman had knocked me cold, let alone a ninety-pound frail like Gwen?

"I must have fainted," I finally said, just to say something. "Where's Dagmar?"

"I told her she is no longer our client."

"All she wanted was to get away."

"But with what?"

I realized that Gwen thought Dagmar had designs on me. Undesirable as Gwen's hankering for me was, it conferred on me a desirability that she might have been alone in noticing. But she assumed every other woman was after me as well. Perhaps a case could be made for this . . .

I was distracted from this pleasant line of thought by Gwen's review of what had happened. Dagmar had come to see me after Brunswick had mentioned my name. She left a sports bag full of explosives when she and Gwen went to the john.

"The kidnapping was obviously staged. Those two men were her accomplices."

"In what?"

She closed her eyes and shook her head. "I refuse to think about it. That girl will come to no good, but she is no longer our client."

A chance of redemption glimmered on the horizon of my still wobbly mind. Gwen had put a lot into that punch. My manner misled her. She had no idea how humiliated I felt at having been struck by my partner. Thanks God she had hit Dagmar first. Had there been any witnesses? It didn't matter. I knew. Obviously I couldn't hit her back. The risk was too great. Gwen was belted in several oriental martial arts. But could she walk barefoot on a man's back? My revenge was clear. I must remain Dagmar's champion and exonerate her from the charges that thus far only Gwen had made but which Brunswick too might level at her. Dagmar deserved the best and I was at her disposal.

Lying back, I sighed and closed my eyes.

"Does it still hurt?"

"I need more rest."

"Of course." Her warm hand fluttered to my face, patted my forehead. "You have a temperature."

"Doesn't everyone?"

She never laughed at my jokes but she laughed then. Her guilt went deep. I heard her leave the room.

It was my turn to review recent events. Dagmar had come to me out of fear of Derringer, but now Derringer was dead. Like me, Dagmar had been taken into custody, and the reason for that was as flimsy as the reason for arresting me. Just because I was found in a ladies' room with a gun in my hand and the bullet riddled body of Derringer enthroned in a booth. I had been shoved into the room by a man whose face I would never forget. I had seen his first cousin in the Museum of Science's display representing the stages of evolution. Obviously Dagmar had been similarly shoved in there. That was when Brunswick was called. In the meantime, I showed up and was propelled in where Dagmar was being detained with the murdered body of her employer. The explanation was risibly obvious.

A civil war had broken out in Derringer's organization and Dagmar had been caught in the middle. The attempt to frame her was crude, but her enemies might be attracted to it in the future. I had to talk with her.

In order to do this, I had to give Gwen the slip. Nothing easier. I dressed quietly and crept to the door. I put my ear against it and listened. Was Gwen out there? There was the soft murmur of the television. Television always put her to sleep. I gripped the door handle and turned slowly, then pushed. Nothing. The door was locked.

I mastered the impulse to beat on the door. That would have wakened Gwen, brought her on the run, and postponed my visit to Dagmar. It was a ten-foot drop from my window to a balcony below. I did not hesitate. I crossed the room and beat on the door.

I heard her scramble to the door and fumble with the key. In a moment, the door swung open and she rushed to the bed where I had drawn the covers over deceptively arranged pillows. I scooted around the door and outside and pulled the door closed. It gave me immense satisfaction to turn the key in the lock. Two can play at that game.

Gwen's Bronco was in the parking lot below and I borrowed the keys from her bag. There was an "Andy of Mayberry" rerun on television but I tore myself away. Below in the parking lot, as I was getting behind the wheel of the Bronco, I looked up. Gwen was hanging from my window. Then she dropped onto the terrace below. I started the engine and got out of there.

Several blocks away, I pulled into a Burger King to use the public phone. There was no directory and I stood in line impatiently to ask one of the employees for it.

"Do you have a directory?"

"Large or small."

"Chicago."

133

"Does that mean large?"

"Of course."

She rolled her eyes patiently. "Fries?"

"Fries!"

She made a face and punched at her computer. "That will be $2.98."

"For a telephone directory!"

"You want to eat in a booth?"

"I want the manager."

There was impatient rumbling in the line behind me. I sensed that sympathy was with the clerk and not with me. Behind her an adenoidal chap with lidded eyes appeared.

"I'm the manager."

"I want to use the phone."

"Go ahead."

"I don't know the number."

"Call information."

This was spoken into a silence that had formed. I felt at a disadvantage. "What's your name?" I asked, trying to sound menacing, but I found myself being pushed away from the counter as the hungry hordes pressed forward. I slunk to the phone, hearing behind me a voice crying that I owed $2.98. I called information.

"Do you have the number of a Milosovich?"

"Which one?"

"Anyone."

"I've got two and a half columns of Milosovichs."

"Is there a Mary?"

"There are eight M. Milosovichs."

I had a sudden inspiration. "Give me the number of Transfiguration Church."

"You're kidding."

"Why do you say that?"

"It's been in the papers and on television. The place has been shut down."

"Transfiguration?"

"That's right."

"How do you shut down a church?"

"Well, first you have to be made cardinal . . ."

I put down the phone. I turned and faced the man with the jack o'lantern smile. "Mertz wants to see you."

"I don't know any Mertz."

"I'll introduce you."

Once more I felt a knifepoint in my belly. He indicated the exit. In the lot, he prodded me toward a familiar vehicle.

"I wondered what happened to my car."

"So did I. You ever have the thing serviced?"

"At its age?" But it was pointless to expect this dolt to catch the witty reference to animal husbandry. "Do you want me to drive?"

"If you can get it started."

The Bronco would be safe in the Burger King lot. The place was open twenty-four hours a day. Like one of the late Derringer's skin joints. The car did not start immediately. If it had, I could have gotten away without my escort, since he lumbered around the car when I got behind the wheel. Of course I had my own key. Jack O'Lantern was in the passenger seat when I pulled away.

Mertz was a cadaverous man whose physiognomy had destined him for the undertaking trade. But there he was in a windowless office at the rear of one of the late Derringer's sleazier joints, wearing suit and tie, his long ringless fingers intertwined upon the top of his desk. He stood when I was in the room, but remained slightly bowed. Perhaps he had put in time running one of the oriental massage parlors. I bowed in return. Then I realized it was the low ceiling that explained Mertz's posture.

135

The reader with experience in copyediting will scrawl a query in the margin: *How does Slattery know this is Mertz?* Those familiar with the logical demands of such a reader will realize that it will not do simply to say that Jack O'Lantern had come to take me to Mertz, we had gotten into my car and driven away, presumably to see Mertz. Ergo, the man behind the desk must be Mertz. That requires too much offstage thinking on the part of the reader. No problem. There is a nameplate on the desk, facing me, reading Basil Mertz. To placate the copyeditor, I will have Mertz reach out with his long fingers and line the nameplate up with the edges of the desk's surface. This will establish that he is a meticulous man.

"You are Slattery," he said.

"And you are Mertz."

"Mr. Mertz."

I looked around the office. "I don't see your wife here."

Behind me, there was the sound of gurgling a clogged coffee machine will give off as it forces hot water through its calcified passages. Mertz's eyes lifted to my escort and the giggling stopped.

"Wait outside, Jack."

"Is that his real name?"

"John."

"Ah."

I was finding Mertz hard to figure. In the wake of Derringer's murder, there was the danger of full-scale civil war breaking out among his erstwhile cronies. The capo had been killed; there would be little hesitation eliminating anyone else who stood in the way. But stood in the way of whom? Was Mertz seeking control or only wanting to survive until it was clear whose boot he should lick? I put a version of this two-pronged question to him.

"I will not work for a woman."

"Then you aren't married?"

No gurgle this time. Jack was gone and Mertz's sense of humor seemed to have atrophied years ago.

"Derringer gave her the name of Dagmar West. He thought she was just a cute blow-up doll. Not that he didn't put her on the regular schedule. Within a year, she is plotting to take over."

I kept a straight face. Did Mertz know I had met Dagmar, in my office, in the ladies' room, at police headquarters? Evidently not. He went on to speak of Dagmar as a hardhearted hoofer with ambitions far beyond the dreams of avarice.

"Who said that?"

He looked around the office as if to make sure we were alone. "I did."

"I meant the phrase, 'dreams of avarice.' "

"One of the nuns in school used it."

"One of the nuns."

"I attended the parish school. Transfiguration."

Was this a test? I looked wise, what Gwen calls my gastro-intestinal expression. "They closed it down."

He sighed, then splayed one of his long fingered hands across his narrow chest. "Not in here."

"What did you want to see me?"

"You're a private dick, aren't you?"

I smiled. So I did have a reputation after all. "I am."

"What do I do to hire you?"

"Pay me money."

"I meant how much?"

"That depends on why you want to hire me."

He took his hand from his breast, waved away my presumed suspicions, laid it on the desk with the other one.

"It's all legit. I want you to nail Dagmar for the death of Derringer."

Clearing the way for him to ascend the throne? But I could not imagine the waif-like Dagmar involved in this kind of high stakes power move. It was clear that, whatever his motive, Mertz wished Dagmar ill. So did Gwen.

"The police have already let her go."

"I know. I had Jack switch guns before we put Dagmar in the john."

"You!"

"I thought she was innocent. Now I know better."

"How?"

"She's trying to frame me."

What a tangled web we had here, and it didn't matter that it existed only in Mertz's mind. What currents were running in the Derringer organization? How many were vying for the top job?

"Only a handful," Mertz said when I asked him. "And Dagmar. She's a handful in herself."

I bristled, but he apparently meant no double entendre. My adolescent desire to protect Dagmar's body and name from the predators of the organization into which she had been deceptively introduced so short a time ago filled me with heroic zest. It occurred to me that the best way to protect her interests was to be in the hire of her enemies.

"I'll need a hundred as a retainer."

He hesitated, sat forward, glanced at a picture hanging on the wall. *Whistler's Mother.* "I can only give you fifty."

I nodded. "It's the principle of the thing."

Mertz stood, moved *Whistler's Mother* on her hinges, twirled a dial and opened a small wall safe. He reached in and brought out a package. He closed the safe, restored the painting and sat at the desk where he proceeded to count out bills. Thousands. He counted fifty of them and pushed them toward me. I tried to recover my gastro-intestinal expression, but this was difficult. I had never been given such a wad in my life. I stood with the money in my hand.

"I'll be going."

"Better put that cash away."

Where does one put fifty thousand-dollar bills? I loosened my belt and slipped them into my shorts. Mertz pushed his chair back from the desk as if I were about to flash.

"Where is the gun that shot Derringer?"

He shrugged. "In the briny deep?"

"Who said that?"

"Popeye."

5

At Jack's suggestion, I had parked my car in the next block.

It was now the center of a small crowd, two patrol cars, and an ambulance. The trunk door was raised and a cop and a paramedic were bent over, looking in. I edged closer, hoping I wouldn't be recognized. The paramedic straightened and backed away.

"He's dead."

"So take him to the morgue."

"The union won't allow it. Call the meat wagon."

The paramedic weaved his way through the crowd to the ambulance. The cop stepped back too and I got a chance to peer into my trunk. Staring upward through lifeless eyes was the man who had hustled me to the ladies' room in the Ooo la la.

I found a public phone at a filling station at the corner.

"Gwen? Ish. Did you report my car stolen?"

"I reported mine stolen," she said coldly.

"It's in the parking lot at the Burger King."

"I was hoping they'd arrest you driving it and I could deny I ever knew you." And she burst into tears.

Poor wounded bird. A woman is never so vulnerable as when she has revealed her hand. This was as close as Gwen had come to declaring her passion for me, but I understood. What man would not? Oh, to have her brain and heart housed in a structure like Dagmar's. But would she love me then? Her imagined fickleness made me brisk.

"Go get the Bronco at Burger King and pick me up at . . ." I crouched and looked through the murky window to see what the street sign said. I read it off to Gwen.

"I'll be there."

"When are you not?"

I waited inside the station until I saw the Bronco moving tentatively along the curb. I ran out and hopped in.

"Let's get out of here."

"Where to?"

The office? Mine looked like a suite in Sarajevo but Gwen's was unscathed. A little ripple of resentment rode over the surface of my soul.

"Your office," I growled.

"Ish, it's ours, not mine."

"That's true."

Gwen paid the rent on the whole suite now, so I could lay as much claim to her room as mine. I was silent as she drove, chattering as she did. Compulsive talking was not like her. To quiet her I told her I had accepted Mertz as a client.

"Mertz?"

"He wants me to prove that Dagmar was taking over an operation that had been run by a gang of cutthroats for years."

"Did he give you any leads?"

"Leads! The whole idea is preposterous."

"Then why did you take the job?"

I looked at my meatless partner huddled over the wheel of her Bronco. She had the profile of a thirteen-year-old boy, with chest to match. "I specialize in lost causes," I said.

"We'll get the goods on Dagmar West. I guarantee it."

I reflected that at the moment Dagmar was probably taking the goods off in one of the smoky clubs the one-time Derringer organization ran. Two men were dead, she had been arrested, one of the top bananas had hired me to make a case against Dagmar, but she would be up on that rhythmic runway taking it all off because the show must go on. The little girl from Transfiguration had grit, no doubt about that.

She was waiting for us in Gwen's office.

At first I didn't recognize her. Her fuchsia raincoat had a hood which she had pulled over her head. She wasn't wearing her blonde wig either. Even her bosom seemed diminished. She noticed me staring.

"Cheap back-alley silicone," she said.

False? I had the fleeting notion that with a little help Gwen could blossom like Dagmar. The body as reshapeable mass. But then Dagmar flung back the hood and her uplifted chin and the fire in her eye brought back the girl who had taken my breath away the first time she walked into my office.

"I've been waiting here for hours."

"How did you get in?"

"Through the door."

"Wasn't it locked?"

"Sure. A Yale. A piece of cake."

"Do you remember the man who pushed me into the

ladies' room with you at the Ooo la la?"

"Reuben?"

"He's dead. Someone put him into the trunk of my stolen car."

"You stole a car?"

Gwen made a noise. "Is that all you have to say?"

"It sounds like Mertz."

"Why do you say that?" I asked encouragingly, slipping into the chair at Gwen's desk. "Is there coffee, Gwen?"

She glared at me. "We just this moment got here."

"I thought I smelled coffee."

"You do," Dagmar said. "I made it. I hope you don't mind."

"Why aren't you drinking some?" Gwen asked.

"I made it for Mr. Slattery."

"Call me Ishmael," I urged. "Gwen, let's all have a cup."

"I never drink coffee," Dagmar said primly.

She did accept a fruit drink Gwen kept in the little fridge in the corner of her office. Holding her paper cup in both hands, legs crossed, leaning forward to give the silicone full advantage, she spoke musingly.

"Reuben dead, and Mr. Derringer. It is what everyone feared, a hostile takeover."

"By whom?"

"By any of three men. Reuben. And the man you described as accosting you at the outdoor telephone."

"Jack O'Lantern?"

She laughed. "He used to play hockey. Without a mask. He's not as dumb as he looks. And of course Mertz."

"He thinks you should be added to the list," Gwen said.

"I know. Jack told me that, but I didn't believe him. Not until the explosion here. Mertz gave me that sports bag.

When I asked why it was so heavy, he said it contained one of his bowling trophies. I should have been suspicious then. Mertz doesn't bowl."

"Who was the man who kidnapped us?" Gwen asked.

"That was Reuben."

"Who was Jack O'Lantern working with?"

"I don't know."

"They all said they worked for Derringer."

"They all did. While he was still alive."

"Mertz tried to hire me."

"Don't you work for me?"

"Of course he does," Gwen said, surprisingly. "Your fate is in the competent hands of Ishmael Slattery."

"And associates?" I suggested.

Before the silence grew uncomfortable, the phone rang. Gwen beat me to it. But almost immediately she handed the phone to me.

"Brunswick."

"What's up, Brunswick?" I was gratified by Dagmar's trilling laughter. Sycophancy is one thing, appreciation is another. Not that Gwen was laughing. Her expression suggested that my gastro-intestinal look was contagious.

"We found your car, Slattery."

"Oh good."

"There was a body in the trunk."

"No."

"That's two, Slattery. What's going on at Derringer's clubs?"

"Most people go there to see what's coming off."

"I want you down here pronto, Slattery."

"I don't have a car."

"I've sent one for you."

"Is this an arrest?"

"Call it what you want, but when you abandon your car with the body of a man you claim has been harassing you, I think I have a professional obligation to talk to you."

"Let me put you on with my social secretary."

I handed the phone to Gwen. She listened for a moment, then put it down. "He hung up."

"They're coming for me."

"Why?"

"Because a dead Reuben was found in my car."

Gwen sprang to her feet and pulled me to mine. "You've got to get out of here." She hesitated. "Both of you. Come on."

She hustled us into the hallway and then, on a dead run to the back stairway at the top of which she squeezed my hand. "Don't go to your place." A pained look and then a reconsideration. "Maybe Dagmar should stay here."

"And get arrested again? Not on your life." And she went bouncing down the stairs like a bag full of beach balls with myself in hot pursuit, so to speak.

"Call," Gwen called plaintively after us.

I stopped Dagmar before she opened the door into the parking lot. I nodded for her to follow me, and went down another flight to the basement. From windows there we had a view of the parking lot. My plan was simple. Wait for the police to come and go up to my office, then exit with Dagmar and take off in the Bronco.

Our patience was soon rewarded and then we doubled back to the exit door and moved swiftly as fog on little cat feet to the Bronco.

"Oh I love these," Dagmar squealed.

Moments later we were motoring away to a destination as yet undecided. "We can't go to my place."

She looked at me through the lattice work of her heavily

made up lashes. "Will you behave if we go to mine?"

"I am a licensed detective," I said indignantly. Private dick had always seemed redundant to me. I felt a surge of professional self-abnegation. "We'll go to my partner's place."

Dagmar was not prepared for the pastel chintz nest Gwen had made for herself on the top floor of an exclusive apartment building on the north shore.

"She doesn't look at all like this."

"You don't know her soul."

"She must be a great help to you."

I chuckled. "I think of her as an apprentice. She did clerical work at an agency I was affiliated with before forming my own."

"But she's your partner."

"Look around," I suggested. "She has the money. That was important at the beginning, before the clients came clamoring. It would be churlish now to ask her to go."

Dagmar was silent for a moment. "Inspector Brunswick told me that you worked for Gwen."

My laughter was half convincing. "Ah, what envy will do to an otherwise good man. Poor Brunswick. But imagine what it must be like, harassing former colleagues, retrieving stolen cars, dropping the bodies of hoodlums off at the morgue. Would you care for a drink?"

"They killed him, Slattery. Mertz and Jack. Reuben told me they were plotting against Derringer and he had warned the boss."

"Why did he tell you that?"

"He liked me," she said simply.

That made sense, I supposed. The taciturn, ruthless second-echelon hoodlum needs someone to tell his troubles to. The naive unthreatening Dagmar would be perfect for the role. But where had such confiding taken place? There were many details of Dagmar's life that I realized I would never know—or want to know. But the image of her being whispered to by the late Reuben filled me with a sudden devil-may-care outlook. Dagmar was a lovely thing, but the sport of a moment, a toy. Enjoy her while you may, I recommended to myself, then fling her from you like a crushed grape.

"Wine?" she asked, pouring out two glasses.

"That's grape juice. There's nothing alcoholic here."

"I knew Gwen was a kindred spirit."

"You have a lot in common."

"A sound mind in a sound body."

"Well, there's nothing wrong with her mind."

Dagmar looked at me sadly. "Do you really think that looks matter, an extra pound here, a curve there, a pretty face? Most of it's phony, Slattery. It's what's up here that counts."

I followed her hand from bosom to forehead. Oddly, this made me dizzy. But I should be used to her endowments by now. She went on, speaking of her lifelong ambition to be an intellectual, to wear thick glasses and be listened to when she spoke. Prancing around in the nude was a humiliation, she said. She despised herself for doing it and hated those who had conned her into the life.

Her words were as soporific as an intellectual's. I found myself feeling a powerful desire to go to sleep. The thought of lying down on the floor was irresistible. I stood to do so and then fell gently into oblivion.

6

In the Sunday supplements of my youth one came upon articles dealing with people buried alive. Out of suspicion, perhaps, or only by accident, the victim was dug up and there were the gory results of awaking six feet under, boxed in, air running out. Torn throats and other evidence of loss of air were not what sent a chill down my spine. It was the psychological terror, the realization that one was trapped beyond rescue, the end inevitable. It never occurred to me that the darkness would add to the fright.

I awoke in circumstances that brought forcibly back to me these lurid and sensational stories. My limbs were not bound, I was not lying in a plush coffin, there was an edge of light to the darkness. I put out my hand and it struck metal. Metal that gave under the pressure of my hand. The crack of light widened to a wedge and then let in the whole out of doors. I was in a car trunk. When I sat up there was a burst of applause.

Looking around, I saw that those clapping were for the most part uniformed. But it was a silhouette in civvies that came toward me.

"We got a call that you would be in there."

It was Brunswick who spoke. It emerged, after I emerged, that I was in the police lot reserved for recovered stolen cars. The car I had been in was my own.

"I got a call that the car would be here," I said.

"You also got a call that I was sending a car for you."

"Where are the keys?"

"Not in the trunk."

My thoughts of course were on Dagmar. If I had been stashed in the trunk of my car at police headquarters, what had they done with her? Not that Brunswick was inclined to let me go without an explanation of what had happened. My hurried narrative that I had been anxious to save the taxpayers' money and had taken a bus to pick up my car met with skepticism. Brunswick was convinced that I had wanted to see if something I had hidden in my car was still there.

"A body?" I asked.

147

"Did you put Reuben there?"

I humored him, of course. Once he knew I was anxious to leave, he would keep me there indefinitely. There was, after all, the inconvenient fact that a dead body had been found in the trunk of my car. A trunk into which I myself had been subsequently lodged. I shivered at the thought of sharing a resting place with the late Reuben.

After a cup of coffee in Brunswick's office, my head began to clear.

"What are you on?" he asked.

"Someone doctored our drinks."

"Gwen too? That's funny, she's reported a missing Bronco. Does the Bronco have a trunk?"

I ignored his feeble efforts at humor. This was no time to worry about Gwen and her pardonable pique at my purloining her Bronco. I had a client to consider. Yes, a client. Accepting the fifty thousand from Mertz had been a ruse. The fifty thousand. I patted my pockets. I had finally managed to get the wad into the inner pocket of my corduroy sports jacket, but it was no longer there. Where had I been since receiving the money? Put off by the discovery of Reuben in my trunk, I had telephoned Gwen to come for me, which she did. At the office, Dagmar awaited us. After some time, I had gone off with Dagmar, borrowing the Bronco and taking Dagmar to Gwen's apartment, as the least likely place where we would be sought. I had been wrong. The money must have been in my pocket when Dagmar and I were slipped a mickey. But by whom? The thought grew in me that Dagmar was still at Gwen's, or at any rate out of harm's way. How she had accomplished it I knew not, but I was convinced that Gwen was the author of my present ignominy. Did she keep a pitcher of spiked punch in the fridge just in case? It would be like her, foolish female, to drive me to the police lot, dump me in the trunk of my car, and then call Brunswick to tell him where I could be found. Reporting the Bronco as missing was an unnecessary grace note.

"I'm going," I told Brunswick, settling my feet on the floor and rising slowly.

"On one condition."

I waited.

"Get that car out of our lot."

A block away, I was hailed by Dagmar, who stepped suddenly out of the recessed entryway of a clinic. I pulled over and she opened the passenger door which swung free. I called a warning but she moved fast and got out of its way.

"Just get in and buckle up," I said. "The door will close itself when I get going."

Well, not quite. She grabbed it and pulled it shut. Her bosom, outlined by these exertions, seemed if possible even more ample than I remembered.

"What happened?"

She waved away the recent past as if it were a mere bagatelle. Not to be outbid by such magnanimity, I told her we had been undone by my partner.

"Why?"

"Jealousy."

"Professional?"

"That too."

"Jealous of you and me?" She laughed.

I made a deprecating face and shrugged. "Where to?"

"Do you know where Transfiguration parish is?"

"Tell me."

I followed her directions and we wound up in a little street that time forgot. It was lined on both sides by rows of neat bungalows. At the corner a church the size of a cathedral rose above the trees. Behind it was the school. There was also a convent and rectory. She directed me to pull up before the rectory. We had come, she told me, to pay a visit on the pastor.

"I'll wait."

"No, come in with me."

His name was Father Cap, though this was short for something long that ended in ski. He wore a buttoned soutane, and sparse spears of still-red hair were drawn carefully across the globe of his head. Told that his visitor was Mary Milosovich, a graduate of the parish school, his wariness diminished. His old parishioner done up as Dagmar would have given any celibate pause.

"Ah, Milosovich. Of course, of course. I buried both your parents."

Dagmar nodded and we all observed a moment of silence.

"You broke your parents' hearts, child."

"I wanted to make something of myself."

"And what would that be?"

"I wanted money, fame, excitement."

"And have you got them?"

"No."

"What was the man's name again?"

"It doesn't matter."

"Tell him," I urged, surprising them both. They seemed to have forgotten I was there. This knack for invisibility is, you will appreciate, invaluable in my line of work.

"Mertz," Dagmar said in a whisper. "Basil Mertz. He promised me everything."

"Marriage?"

"He has a wife."

The old priest scrubbed his face with both hands. What must life look like from his vantage point, I wondered. Vanity fair, a ship of fools, a vale of tears. Not too far from the mark, by and large. But why had Dagmar brought me here to hear this tale of woe? It occurred to me that it did not jibe with the story she had given me when she first sailed into my office. Then the villain of the piece was Derringer. To her priest, she confided that it was the treacherous Mertz who had lured her from the innocent confines of Transfiguration parish into a low life of cigar smoke, loud music and dancing in the buff.

"Mertz told me he was from Transfiguration," I said.

"A lie," Dagmar said. "Apparently he thought I had not confided in you completely and the reference to Transfiguration would be clue enough for you."

I nodded in the manner of one who did not need half so much to get his inquisitive juices flowing. Not that I had made anything in particular out of Mertz's remark, except to think that it is a small world.

"Why have you come to me?" Father Cap asked.

"To see if you would see me."

"The nuns always said you would come to a bad end, Mary."

"I know."

"Do you want to go to confession?"

He glanced at me and I was immediately on my feet. So was Dagmar. "Not this time, Father." She took something from her purse. "Would you keep this for me?"

"What is it?"

"Money."

He shook his head sadly. His expression indicated what he thought the source of the money was. It occurred to me that the package she held out to the priest was the fifty thousand I had gotten from Mertz.

"It's okay, Father," I said. "The money's mine."

"And what do you do?"

"I am a private investigator." I added, "I was in the police force for some time."

A cop. That made a difference. He took the money, turned in his chair and bent over to open the parish safe. When it was safely stored, he stood, smiling.

"Call for it within a month or it becomes a donation to the parish."

"Wasn't Transfiguration shut down?" I asked Dagmar in the car.

"Don't you read the papers?"

She sounded like Gwen. "What do they say?"

"The campaign to keep it open was successful. There is a fund drive underway to make necessary repairs to the church."

In the light of such a project my ill-gotten fifty thousand was not much, but it was the biggest fee I had ever commanded and I intended to get it back. Thank God I had been there when Dagmar handed over the cash and had the chance to identify it as my own.

"You should have told him it was mine," I chided.

"Would he have believed me?"

"Where to?"

"The Papiti."

I glanced at her. The Papiti was where I had talked with Mertz and taken his fifty thousand dollars. It did not seem the part of wisdom for me to show up now with the woman he had accused of conspiring to take over the late Derringer's operation. But it seemed even less wise for Dagmar to walk in there alone.

"I can handle him."

There did seem to be a new strength in the girl. Perhaps her moral batteries had been charged by the visit to her home parish.

"What will you tell him?"

"That he has nothing to fear from me."

I dropped her at a corner where she disappeared inside a

dress shop. My throat thickened at the trouble she was taking to disassociate me from her confrontation with Mertz. I circled the block, a protective patrol, but as I came again along the street I was startled to see Gwen walking purposefully toward the Papiti. I turned away as I drove past her and then headed for home.

My apartment has the look of an office, largely because I had worked out of it when I was getting started as an independent private investigator. I sat at my desk, put a blank sheet of paper before me, and put the pieces together.

What the police wanted was whoever had killed Derringer and Reuben. It was not that they regretted the passing of these two, but it was not good policy to permit private citizens to do the justice system's work for it. To say nothing of encouraging an unchecked gang war. My own aim was to free Dagmar from the clutches of the crowd she had all innocently fallen in with. Her manner had been palpably different when we sat in the pastor's office at Transfiguration. I could imagine her going straight again. Not completely straight, of course. What a vision she must be walking barefoot on the back of a man who knew how to appreciate her. I dismissed from my mind as unworthy of the subject Gwen's predictable objections to a close friendship between Dagmar and myself. Not that I could get all that close, given her pectoral amplitude.

I stared at the blank paper. Who had killed Derringer and Reuben? It was risible to imagine that it had been Dagmar. Reuben had shoved her into the john with the dead capo just as he had me. Reuben had killed Derringer, I decided, and then tried to frame Dagmar. Mertz's claim to have switched weapons drew attention to him. Reuben had been killed with the same weapon Derringer had.

I picked up the phone and dialed Brunswick.

"Who should I say is calling?"

"Mrs. Derringer."

"But you're a man."

"I'm her houseboy."

Silence. "Just a minute."

"Slattery?" Brunswick said, coming on. "What the hell is it now?"

"How are you coming on the Derringer and Reuben killings?"

"Do you want to confess?"

I thought of Father Cap and smiled. "Later. Have you found the murder weapon?"

"Where did you hide it?"

"I would guess it is at the bottom of the Chicago River."

"Which bridge?"

"Brunswick, I am prepared to solve your case."

"I know. Gwen told me. I'm to come to the Papiti Club in half an hour. Are you calling from there?"

"Just be sure you're there."

I hung up. I smiled. Gwen had been working with me so long she was able to anticipate my thoughts. Like a master magician with his apprentice, I wondered if I had taught her too much. But of course it did not take genius to see that I would be putting the finger on Mertz. I only wished that Dagmar could be there for the scene in which the master did his stuff. Would Mertz crack and confess or would there be violence? I swallowed. Brunswick would come prepared.

7

He did indeed. He had with him detectives Plague, Famine, Pestilence and War, as the four were called. They had won their spurs as horsemen on the mounted police detail. Their switch to the detective bureau was precipitated by their unwillingness to ride horses equipped with a baggie behind, an equine diaper. As detectives they were good horsemen, but they were big and they wore forbidding expressions, actually the frown of the uncomprehending which the uninstructed read as menacing. There were several patrol cars parked in the lot of the club and I saw Gwen's Bronco as well. I pulled in beside it and hopped out.

"Your motor's running," a patrolman called.

"I know. It's hard to get started again."

I walked jauntily to the club entrance, pulling the brim of my hat even across my eyes. I saluted the patrolman at the door and he took the opportunity to peer inside when he opened the door for me. On the stage the same frenzied dancing went on.

"Why don't you wait inside?" I suggested.

"I'm a married man."

"Then nothing should surprise you."

"Ha."

Brunswick and the Four Horsemen were in Mertz's office. Mertz sat behind his desk, smiling uneasily. Dagmar was in a chair facing him and Gwen fidgeted in the corner. She at least expressed joy at my arrival.

"This is an incompetent private dick named Slattery," Brunswick, always a kidder, announced.

"We've met," Mertz said. "I am Mr. Slattery's client."

Brunswick turned to me. "Is that true?"

"No," Dagmar said indignantly. "I'm his client."

"Mr. Slattery will clarify everything," Gwen said, taking charge. She moved another chair behind the desk, so I was sitting next to Mertz. "Should I begin?"

"Please." What is the point of training someone if you don't give them a chance to shine? In the Middle Ages the master teacher sat enthroned while his apprentices taught; afterward he gave the magisterial solution. So it was with Gwen and myself.

"You're wearing makeup," I whispered to her.

She rubbed at her face, as if in surprise. "Do you like it?"

"Proceed," I suggested.

"You are all wondering why Mr. Slattery asked you here to Mr. Mertz's office at the Papiti Club. The presence of the police is no accident."

Pestilence looked at Famine as if he missed the days when parking violations and the occasional accident defined their duty. My case against Mertz was circumstantial and I hoped Gwen would present it effectively. In any event, I was there to pick up any dropped ball. She continued.

"Two men have met violent deaths in recent days, Derringer the acknowledged owner of a string of strip joints and dubious massage parlors where the girls are little more than slaves, naive young things in from the country and easily sold a bill of goods. The promise of stardom and celebrity is made but it turns out to be little more than a relentless schedule of questionable dancing and unprofessional massage. It is a very lucrative business, most of the income untaxed. The ambitious eye it greedily. Derringer himself rose to the top of the organization after the mysterious death of the previous boss. That boss in turn ascended the throne through an act of violence. It seems reasonable to suppose that the pattern is repeating itself today. And Mr. Slattery has vowed to put an end to it."

I stared fixedly at a painting on the opposite wall, ignoring the curious glances that were cast my way. The painting was difficult to interpret: it could have been a close-up of a rain forest or perhaps some tropical fish. On the other hand . . . But Gwen continued with my findings.

"With Derringer out of the way, the question becomes: Who shall succeed? The demise of Reuben, who may have assassinated Derringer, narrowed the field."

I turned in my chair to look at Mertz. He was following Gwen's narration with rapt attention. His manner suggested that he knew he was soon to be accused of killing Reuben after instigating the assassination of Derringer. If only to prolong Mertz's agony, I interrupted Gwen.

"There are two remaining candidates to take Derringer's place," I observed. "Jack O'Lantern and my putative client, Ed Mertz."

Gwen laughed infectiously. "Mr. Slattery is toying with you. Of course the names he mentioned would occur to anyone. But it is the mark of genius to see what others do not see. Shall I reveal the culprit, Mr. Slattery?"

I nodded at Gwen, tugging a Lucky from the crushed packet I still carried. Gwen turned and pointed dramatically at Dagmar.

"There is your murderer, Inspector Brunswick. Mary Milosovich!"

All heads turned to the sumptuous blonde in the corner. Dagmar looked disdainfully at Gwen.

"She came to Mr. Slattery at Inspector Brunswick's inspired suggestion, bringing a tale of abuse and exploitation by the Derringer organization. And so it might have begun. But young Mary Milosovich had become fascinated by the career of a former fellow parishioner, an older man who was regularly pointed to as one who had chosen the broad road to destruction rather than the narrow gate of salvation. Mary envied rather than despised the man she heard about. But how could a woman emulate such a career? To do so she must use a woman's wiles. The Lord had given her the body, but had been less lavish elsewhere."

Gwen moved swiftly to Dagmar and snatched at her hair. To my astonishment her blonde tresses came away in Gwen's hand. On Dagmar's head a small crop of mouse colored hair sprouted. But Gwen was not done. Deftly she removed the lashes from Dagmar's eyes. With a Kleenex she forcibly removed the lipstick from Dagmar's mouth. The transformation was amazing. The body remained in all its glory but atop it was a most unprepossessing head and a face that seemed as plain as Gwen's. Dagmar, enraged, rose but before she could wreak revenge on Gwen she was detained by Famine and Plague. I too was on my feet, anxious to reverse this miscarriage of justice and correct Gwen's dreadful mistake. But before I could say anything, Dagmar began to speak in a high screeching voice.

"Men are fools! They have no idea what the profits from this organization could be. They are satisfied with the traditional return on investment. Their treatment of dancers and masseuses is a scandalous abuse of capital. A happy stripper is a better stripper, as every woman knows. And they refused to bring in male dancers. The arteries of the organization were clogged with conservative qualms. Within a year I could double income and get twice the mileage out of the dancers."

"So you killed Derringer?"

Her eyes gleamed as had those of stout Cortez when he gazed upon the Pacific. She was caught up in her dream of dominance.

"He killed himself because of his unwillingness to take seriously what I proposed. I had to fight him off while I was explaining my ideas. And Reuben!" Her eyes sparkled with mad anger as she looked at each of us in turn.

"He said he understood. He wanted to hear more. But I knew what he was after. And then when he saw me like this . . ." She waved a hand before her face. "He lost interest in both me and my ideas. When I went to Mr. Mertz, his only suggestion was that I drop the weapon into the Chicago River." Suddenly she produced a nasty looking gun from her purse and pressed the barrel against Gwen's head. "Of course I did no such thing. I may not get out of here alive, but I will take several of you with me. Beginning with this dingbat." And she pressed the barrel painfully against Gwen's head.

A large mistake. Gwen lifted her arm, lifting the gun, and with the other hand brought the blonde wig to Dagmar's face, blinding her. I lunged for the gun but Brunswick beat me to it. In a quince a disarmed Dagmar burst into tears. She tried to focus on me.

"I hate you, I hate you. And I won't pay your bill."

"Good work, Slattery," Brunswick said gruffly, and then he and his comrades were hustling a screaming, resistant Dagmar from the office.

"How much do I owe you, Slattery?" Mertz inquired after emitting a long sigh of relief.

Owe me? I was already into him for fifty grand.

"You'll get a bill," Gwen said. "Mr. Slattery is a stickler for records."

"But I don't want the payment recorded."

"Well, in that case."

He opened his safe and began counting out thousand dollar bills. Gwen let him count them all onto the desk, then scooped them up.

"You won't want a receipt."

"Of course not."

I shook Mertz's hand and then Gwen and I left the office and went through the club. There was a redhead on the runway who was emulating the age old gyrations of passion in a way that even to my jaded eye seemed fetching. Gwen's grip on my arm tightened and we continued to the door.

"How much did Mertz give you?"

"Twice what you stashed in Father Cap's safe."

She had driven a block before it occurred to me to ask how she had known about the money I had left with the pastor of Transfiguration.

"I'll tell you when we get home."

She meant her place. No sooner were we there than she disappeared into her bedroom. A few minutes later, to my utter astonishment, Dagmar West appeared in the bedroom door!

"Dagmar," I cried, unable to suppress the reaction the wench called up in me.

But if the body was the body of Dagmar, the voice was the voice of Gwen. Gwen. With a chest like that, this had to be ventriloquism. How could anyone mistake Dagmar for Gwen? That this was indeed possible when the wig came off, and the lashes, and there undeniably was Gwen. But my eyes were fixed on her chest which had never been so expansive. Indeed, it was the drooling image of Dagmar's. As if in answer to my unstated question, Gwen picked up a pin and stabbed herself. Her bosom burst like a balloon and now there was only familiar flat-chested Gwen. She stepped close to me.

"You didn't recognize me when we went to Transfiguration, did you?"

There are times when silence is the best response. Gwen was moving unnervingly closer. She slipped the blonde wig back on.

"Got any more balloons?" I asked.

SLATTERY WINNER

1

What kind of a mother would call me Ishmael? Since I wasn't consulted, I can't say. The only Ishmael she ever knew was in the family Bible. Nonetheless, it is the name to which I answer, as I did that hot August morning when Gwen Probst called.

"Are you sitting down?"

"I had to get up to answer the phone. What else is up?"

"I'm getting married."

I observed a moment of silence, consulting my feelings. They were mixed. On the one hand, I had always assumed that Gwen had designs on me. On the other hand, in the web of skin between forefinger and thumb, I have a design put there by a one-eyed tattoo artist in San Diego. A postage stamp size skull and crossbones. Don't ask me for details.

"Married," I finally said.

"And I want you to be there."

"Best man?"

"Groom."

"Where you calling from, Weenie's?"

Weenie's specialty was hot dogs, but most people went there to drink.

"My head is clear as a bell."

"You better check your clapper, then. You're the second phone call this morning."

"What's up?"

161

I sat down again. "A man wants me to provide security for his lottery ticket."

"A winner?"

"The next drawing is on Saturday." It was now Thursday morning.

"I'll bet he offered to share his winnings."

"How'd you know?"

"Ish, demand cash on the barrel head."

"Have you any idea what the lottery is worth this week?" It had passed thirty million before the Wednesday drawing and if it carried over to Saturday it might double that amount.

"I know what a losing ticket's worth."

"You have no spirit of adventure."

"Would I work with you if I didn't? What did you tell him?"

"He'll be here in half an hour."

"Stall him till I get there."

The phone slammed in my ear. I slammed my own in response, missed the cradle, and jammed my thumb in the bargain. Pain shot up my arm, then returned to my thumb. It hurt too much to cry. It might have been Gwen's revenge for my refusing to play groom to her bride.

Gwen is my partner in Slattery & Probst, Private Investigations (a phrase subject to ribald interpretations), having finally talked me into double billing. If I am a PI she is the square root thereof. Still, she is useful to me in my work. Given the relative mental capacities of male and female, she could never be my equal, of course, as I am not loath to tell her.

"You're right about that," she said with an evil smile. "Less can never equal more."

Maybe that's why we get along. She knows her place. And she's nuts about me.

★ ★ ★ ★ ★

As I waited, I ignored my throbbing head, nibbled on my nails and reviewed the first telephone conversation of the morning.

"This Slattery?" a male voice had said.

"Who's asking?"

"You're a detective?"

"That's what it says on the sign."

"I need help."

This is the moment psychiatrists, priests and parole officers know—a fellow human being in trouble. My forehead felt pasty when I rubbed it. "Tell me all about it."

"I want you to hold a lottery ticket for me."

"Is it heavy?"

"It's hot. I've been threatened."

"Threatened?" I am not one who advances on trouble with steely eyes and squared jaw. There was panic in the man's voice.

"I'm coming to see you," he said.

"Can you afford it?"

"When I collect my winnings I'll split." An amphibolous remark, but he seemed too scared to be playing word games.

"What's your name?"

"Walter Benjamin."

That was all. As I sat there, I regretted having told Gwen of the call. Why would someone with a lottery ticket be in danger? Of course, I was assuming that it was a ticket for the Saturday drawing. Suddenly, as it does to few men, the epiphany came. It had to be a ticket for the Wednesday drawing! A thirty-million-dollar pot. A spasm of dizziness came and went. Any fraction of that and I would no longer

163

depend on Gwen's inheritance to keep the office open during lean periods. There would be no point in keeping the office open at all.

In the window, the air-conditioner wheezed and rattled, as if seeking a reason for going on. Earlier, it had seemed a metaphor for my life. Ishmael Slattery, loser. I had spent the night in the office and when I awoke and stumbled to my desk, the air-conditioner and I were considering the purpose of life. My mind had seemed a computer screen across which a message endlessly passed. *You will soon know good luck.* This chuckle-headed reassurance had been pulled from a fortune cookie. I had tried without success to believe it. Now I did.

The putative client arrived before Gwen. There was a knock on the door, I called, "Come in," the door opened and I was looking at empty space. Then a hand appeared, gripping the edge of the doorway. There was blood on the hand. A terrible groan, a man teetered into view, advanced into my office, swayed and then fell backward on my office floor. There was a lottery ticket in his bloody hand. He might have been offering it to me. I took it and put it in my shirt pocket.

"You Benjamin?"

He tried to lift his head. He raised it several inches. It was his final effort. His head crashed to the floor and all was still. The driver's license in his wallet indicated that he was indeed, or at least until recently had been, Walter Benjamin. There was a five and four ones in the wallet. I put them with the lottery ticket. And then Gwen arrived.

You never know what a woman will do at the sight of a dead body. Some scream, others faint, yet others go mute with horror. Gwen stepped over the body picked up the phone and dialed 911.

2

The next hours were hectic. The paramedics confirmed that the dead man was dead and put in a call to Frigosso. The coroner, Marlys Frigosso, might have been elected to provide a vivid contrast between the living and the dead. Five feet ten, amply endowed, honey colored hair worn in a ponytail that swished suggestively as she moved and talked, she had my undivided attention. I in turn had Gwen's.

"Well, I guess that's that," Gwen said, trying to propel Frigosso to the door, but the coroner was dead weight.

"You're a private investigator?" she said to me with undisguised interest.

"In the public service."

"I am an avid reader."

"No one's perfect."

She laughed and dug me in the ribs. Gwen, holding a letter opener, looked as if she would like to follow suit. Has anyone ever understood the irresistible attraction some men have for women? There was a rapport between Frigosso and myself that I would have loved to explore, but Gwen was a dampening presence.

"We're partners," Gwen said gruffly, drawing out the word in a way that suggested cohabitation or worse.

"Gwen just told me she's getting married."

"You're Gwen," Frigosso said with maximum disinterest.

"Gwen Probst."

"I'd love to talk to you about your work," Frigosso said to me, a tremolo in her throaty voice.

At that moment, as if to prove that the management of the universe is obscure to mere mortals, Lieutenant Brunswick of the local constabulary arrived. He nodded to the coroner, ignored me and addressed Gwen.

"Who delivered the stiff?" His eyes dropped briefly to the huddled mass of mortality on the floor.

"He arrived under his own power," I said.

"Were you here at the time?" he asked Gwen.

"No."

Brunswick, an old enemy with the cop's contempt for the private investigator, turned to me. "Any witnesses, Slattery?"

"To what?"

"To the way you greeted this poor devil when he arrived."

The lovely Frigosso and I exchanged a smile. I told Brunswick to talk with Gwen and started to lead the coroner into the next room.

"The life of a private investigator is an interesting one," I began, but we were halted by Brunswick who asked the coroner what my visitor had died of.

"As a first guess, I would say the knife in his back did it."

Brunswick turned the body over with the tip of his loafer. A steak knife was indeed embedded in the back of the fallen lottery player.

The phone rang and I beat Gwen to it.

"Slattery?" a muffled voice said.

"Who's speaking?"

"The guy who is going to make hamburger out of you if you don't turn over that lottery ticket."

"Would you care to speak with Police Lieutenant Brunswick?"

The phone was hung up. I handed it to Brunswick any way. He listened to the buzz for a while and then handed it back to me. "Who was it?"

"A wrong number."

Frigosso had activated her crew and my visitor was zipped into a body bag and carried unceremoniously out the door. Brunswick was examining the items he had removed from the dead man's pocket. Eventually, as all things do in this Vale of Tears, the investigation ended. Frigosso left first, throwing me a significant look, and Brunswick, thank God, left some minutes later.

Gwen was seated in the chair behind my desk. My partner in crime. She wore a shapeless dress that matched her figure, a pink plastic barrette in her hair and a pensive look.

"Did you search him for a lottery ticket?" she asked me.

I assumed the air of injured innocence that comes easily to the guilty.

"Give it to me." She held out her unringed left hand.

"If it's a winner, we'll split."

She waggled the fingers of her extended hand. I plucked the lottery ticket from my shirt pocket and gave it to her. "Take care of that for me, will you?"

She took the ticket, stood and swung the portrait of Ayn Rand aside and turned the dial of the safe. Into the opened safe went the ticket, the dial was twirled once more and Ayn Rand swung back into place. The picture was Gwen's contribution to office furnishing. She sat.

"Who would know if a ticket is good before the drawing?" She spoke with the voice of an elementary school teacher.

"Good question."

"One you should have asked yourself. That ticket was for last night's drawing."

"Ah, you noticed that."

"Is it the winning ticket?"

"That's why I wanted you to put it in a safe place."

My insouciance was feigned. Earlier I had felt dizzy when I realized that Benjamin's ticket was a Wednesday winner. With Gwen ensconced at my desk, I imagined zeros receding into infinity, zeros that added up to unimaginable wealth, and now threatened to become an indissoluble bond between my partner and me. How could I plead un-readiness for marriage if I had worldly goods like that to endow her with? But nothing in the gentleman's agreement I had with Gwen required that she share such a bonanza as this. I had to get the ticket back. But caution was the watch-word. It was imperative to get Gwen out of the office so I could open the safe and get that ticket.

"Well," I said. "I'll be going."

"Where?"

"Where does any man go after receiving an expiring potential client?"

"Wash your hands afterward," she said, getting comfort-able in my chair. There was a public phone on the street outside from which I would summon Gwen, thereby getting her out of the office and clearing my way to possession of the ticket. That was the plan.

3

I left the office on tiptoe, lest my cleated heels tell the sharp-eared Gwen that I would be passing the men's room and continuing outside. But before I reached the stairs, a closet door that had not been tightly closed opened and a very large man stepped into the hallway.

"You Slattery?"

There are many answers to that question. You, for instance, would likely answer, "No." I, on the other hand, might say, "Yes. Depending." The Neanderthal who had confronted me with narrow psychopathic eyes was a formidable obstacle to the swift exit I had planned. The tone of his voice did not suggest the disinterested quest for knowledge characteristic of our species. I might nonetheless become his interlocutor. On the other hand, I could beat it back to the office where he would have to confront Gwen who was sufficient to give any man pause.

"Are you a detective?"

Again I hesitated. The likelihood that I could get back to the office without being tackled by my questioner seemed slim.

"Did you call earlier?"

His dumb look was my answer. "I want to hire you," he said.

"I'm terrible busy at the moment."

He stepped closer, blotting out what little light his bulk had previously permitted to seep through from the cloudy window at the end of the hall.

"Someone stole my lottery ticket."

"A winner?"

He gripped my arm tightly and pulled me toward the stairway. "Let's go where we can talk."

Our destination turned out to be Weenie's, which was reassuring. There I was known, if not appreciated. Weenie himself was behind the bar, or the bar was in front of him, the latter a more seemly description since he was the size of a cocktail sausage. I made sure he marked my entry and then followed my burly companion to a booth. Immediately Debbie, a waitress who has been in deep denial for years about her attraction to me, took our order with a preoccupied air.

"What's the matter, lose the lottery?"

"Oh, shut up."

Lottery tickets were sold in Weenie's and a portion of the help's salaries went into the great maw that would soon spew out millions to your favorite private eye. (What is a public eye? Brunswick?) My companion ordered beer and I did the same.

"Did Walter Benjamin call you?"

"Why do you ask?"

"Because the bastard stole my winning lottery ticket."

"Ah."

"My dumbbell sister married him, against my advice."

"And you are?"

"His brother-in-law."

An infinite regress threatened. "Named?"

"It's the name that gets signed to the ticket that counts. And by God it is going to be mine."

He slammed a fist onto the table between us, making the salt and pepper and ketchup jump. Was that the hand that held the steak knife that had been plunged into the back of Walter Benjamin? That would mean he had followed Benjamin to my office and had been waiting in the hallway closet for the officials to depart so that he might confront me.

"You said you wanted to hire me."

"I want you to locate Benjamin and get that ticket."

The urgency with which he spoke suggested limited knowledge of the morning's events. I might have told him that his brother-in-law was no more, but in the circumstances that seemed unwise. Even someone located in the Neolithic Age, mentally, would figure out that I might already have the purloined ticket.

"Do you have a dollar?"

At the moment, Debbie appeared with our beer. My companion paid and from the change selected a dollar and handed it to me.

"Now you are my client," I said, adding it to the trove in my shirt pocket. "Tell me everything about Walter Benjamin."

His account was made more memorable by the bitterness with which he spoke. It was a simple if sordid story. A lottery addict, Horace Munn, for such was his name, had been unable to find time to purchase a ticket to the Wednesday lottery and had entrusted his sister with the task. The lottery was drawn before he picked up his ticket, but his sister had checked the numbers when they were broadcast. She nearly collapsed with excitement, but managed to get the news to Horace. Walter overheard the conversation. When Horace arrived, all atremble to pick up the ticket that would make him a rich man, it and his brother-in-law were gone. On the way to the Benjamin home, Horace had thought benevolent thoughts, deciding to settle a goodly sum on his sister, with the proviso that the money was hers, not Benjamin's. And then he had learned the enraging news. His sister tried to defend her husband against her brother's charge of theft, but there was no other possibility. Benjamin had absconded with the winning ticket. Ever since, Horace had been sleeplessly in search of the perfidious Benjamin.

"And now you have come to me," I said unctuously.

"Did Benjamin call you?"

"Why would you think so?"

"Because I throttled the news out of one of his worthless companions." Horace's powerful hands opened and closed. I cleared my throat.

"And who might that be? I must know everything."

"A scumbag named O'Reilly."

I wrote down this name, but my thoughts were elsewhere. Unbeknownst to Horace, the thief he sought was dead. Equally unknown to him, the ticket was in my office safe. A delicate problem in professional ethics confronted me. How could I keep and cash that ticket without incurring the wrath of Horace Munn, he of the powerful hands who spoke of throttling those who stood in his way?

"I will get on it immediately."

"I'll come with you."

"That isn't the way I work. Your presence might alarm those who otherwise would confide in me."

He scowled as he turned this thought over in his mind, where there seemed scarcely room for it. His hand closed around his glass. For a moment, I thought he was going to crush it, but he lifted it to his mouth and drained its contents. Then he nodded. He borrowed my ballpoint and scrawled a number where he could be reached.

"But this is Weenie's number."

"I'll be waiting here."

4

If the person named O'Reilly had known that Benjamin meant to call on me, he might know more. It was imperative that I go through the motions of an investigation. I did not want the menacing Horace Munn to suspect that what was a mystery to him was not so to me.

I took Gwen's vehicle, mine being low on gas, and while I drove, pondered. How could I cash that ticket without Horace Munn finding out about it? My client had given me the address of his sister and it was there I went.

Letitia Benjamin wore a mournful look. But she could not yet know that she was a widow. If she had, she would doubtless have reacted differently when I told her that her husband had come to see me.

"With the stolen lottery ticket," I added.

"It wasn't stolen."

"But your brother Horace . . ."

She wore what had once been called a wash dress, its floral pattern faded from constant proving of the adjective. Her abundant hair was uncared for, but that was currently the style. Her thin face might have seemed gaunt in the wrong light; I found it patrician. Her long-fingered hands went through a wringing motion, unthreatening, but nonetheless reminding me of her brother's great ham hands with their twitching fingers when he spoke of throttling. Her eyes were the bright orbs of madness—or genius.

"Who is O'Reilly?"

Letitia blushed. "Why do you ask?"

"Horace mentioned him."

"He was the man Horace wanted me to marry. Once I wanted it myself. Until I met Walter."

"I understand that your husband and O'Reilly were friends."

"They are partners, not friends."

The distinction appealed to me, eliciting thoughts of the bony Gwen and her iron will. Letitia told me that Walter Benjamin and Peter O'Reilly were computer consultants.

"Ah."

It was their practice to pool ten dollars each week and buy tickets for every lottery drawing. They had never won a penny before. Horace somehow heard the news and came storming into his sister's home, demanding that she give him the ticket. He would redeem it and distribute the winnings equitably. His own claim was based on many sums borrowed from him by Walter Benjamin. My own claim to the ticket began to seem almost justified. The unwitting widow offered me coffee and I accepted. Talking with her stimulated my thinking. I was beginning to get the picture.

O'Reilly and Benjamin pooled their money to buy lottery tickets. They had bought a winner and Benjamin had decided not to share. He sought to enlist me in his perfidy, wanting me to put the ticket in a safe place. Before he could open the door of my office he had been stabbed in the back. And by who else but his partner, O'Reilly? If Horace Munn had done in his brother-in-law he would not have been lurking around in the hallway. I reviewed my conversation with Munn, but could recall no statement that remotely suggested that he knew Benjamin was dead and was dissembling with me.

"Where could I find Peter O'Reilly?"

"He was here shortly after Walter left."

"Did you tell him where Walter was bound?"

"I didn't know until you told me."

My theory gained support from this. O'Reilly was the man. And Brunswick must be told. It would have been imprudent to use Mrs. Benjamin's phone. In any case, at that moment it rang.

She answered, she listened, all color drained from her face, the phone fell from her hand and she slumped to the floor. No need to guess what she had just learned. I was on my feet, my coffee cup still in my hand. I actually carried it out to my car before I realized it. I tossed it onto the Benjamin lawn, drove a block away and called police headquarters on my cell phone.

"Brunswick?" I asked, having called his private number.

"Who's that?"

"Slattery."

"Where are you?"

Something in his voice suggested caution. I altered my voice. "Is Slattery there?"

"Who is this?"

"Peter O'Reilly. I wish to confess to the murder of Walter Benjamin."

"Slattery, what the hell are you up to?"

I hung up. Either Brunswick recognized my voice or he had made a lucky guess. It occurred to me that, in my office earlier, he had spoken as if I myself might have had something to do with Benjamin's death. I called Gwen.

"Have they arrested you yet?" she asked

"I have broken no traffic laws."

"Ish, Brunswick thinks you did it." She was whispering with great urgency.

"That's nonsense."

"That's what I thought at first."

"At first?"

"He says he has conclusive evidence."

"And you believed him."

Her silence was eloquent.

"*Et tu,* Gweno? If I ever murder anyone, you will be the first to know. You may be the victim. Look, there's something I want you to do."

I laid out my plan with succinctness and cogency. Gwen was to call the state lottery office and tell them that she had bought the winning ticket.

"Ishmael!"

"We will be rich as creases." An odd phrase, one I must look up one day, to see what it means. "And we have as much claim to it as anyone. The owner is dead, murdered by a man who considers himself the co-owner. He does not deserve to profit from his crime. His brother-in-law lied to me, telling me the ticket was really his, bought for him by Benjamin's wife."

"How do you know he lied?"

"The widow Benjamin told me the truth."

"You must tell Brunswick this."

175

"I have. Meanwhile, I want you to make our claim to the ticket."

"Ours?" Her voice grew husky.

"Whither might we not fly with such funds, my love? We can spend the rest of our lives in travel and dissipation."

"And start a family?"

"That too. Dissipation often leads to a family."

It was ungallant of me to trade on Gwen's designs on my body. The only such design I wanted was the tattoo described earlier. But all is fair in love and larceny. If she followed her heart instead of her head, she would do my bidding.

"Make that call, but first sign your name on that ticket, front and back."

"Ish, I am going to search the web for tickets to far-off places."

"Do that."

We hung up. Thoughts of far-off places in pleasant female company put me in mind of Marlys Frigosso. As I dialed the coroner's office, my breath was coming in short pants, something it hadn't done since kindergarten.

5

The smell of formaldehyde is not often thought to be an olfactory delight, nor is the chill air of a morgue normally considered aphrodisiac, but when these are combined with the voluptuous presence of Marlys Frigosso they are both. She wore a smock—it might have been all she wore—sensible heels, but not so sensible that they did not enhance the curvature of her calves. The honey-colored ponytail swished as she turned when I spoke her name. Her green eyes sparked with pleasure.

"Slattery!"

"The same. I had a moment and dropped by because . . ."

But no excuse was necessary. She took my hand and brought me in out of the cold, closing the door of her office where sun shone at the windows and a vase of flowers on her desk emitted perfume.

"Ah, warmth," I said, as if it were not a sweltering August day outside.

"I like it body temperature," she said.

"A live body obviously."

She laughed, pointed to a chair and betook herself around the desk, where she sat and shook a cigarette from a package.

"Do you mind if I smoke?"

"Do you mind if I burn?"

"Oh I'm so glad." She shook the package at me, and I drew forth a long, mentholated filter-tipped cigarette. "Everyone has quit. If they even started."

She lit my cigarette and then her own. I leaned across the desk to draw nearer to the flame of her lighter. The top button of her smock was open and if the plush promise of her flesh was yet left to the imagination, the contrast with the stick figured Gwen was total.

"How I admired your aplomb this morning."

"Ah well."

"And how wise not to mention the lottery ticket."

"Lottery ticket."

"I know all about it." Her expression changed. "My beau is missing."

"Arrows too?"

"Peter O'Reilly."

"How do you know him?"

"We met when he reprogrammed my hard drive."

"The devil."

"He was so excited when he called me about the ticket. Now I can't find him."

"Brunswick is looking for him."

"Why?"

"He never confides in me."

"You must find him. You're a detective. I want to hire you."

"What exactly did O'Reilly tell you about the lottery ticket?"

A gift for narrative is unequally distributed among members of the race, as any investigator will tell you. The relevant point, the significant fact, these are too often lost in a cascade of detail through which only a trained operative can pierce. For all that, it was difficult not to be enthralled with the simple music of Frigosso's voice as she babbled brook-like about the loathsome O'Reilly. She was clearly taken with him. He had a way with coroners as well as computers. My spirit rose at the prospect of rivalry. But the odds were formidable.

One, Marlys Frigosso was not indifferent to Peter O'Reilly.

Two, he had called her with the news that he and Walter Benjamin had won the lottery.

Three, Gwen had noticed my own interest in the coroner and must be kept in the dark about my campaign to enlist the coroner as my companion in far-off pleasure spots.

You might think that the fact that she wanted me to locate O'Reilly was a fourth point. Not at all. Know your enemy, keep him in view—this was elementary strategy.

"Can you give me any leads?"

She had lit another cigarette and a great cumulus cloud formed above her golden head. She seemed to be considering her answer. After the effusive torrent of words to which I had just been treated, this was noteworthy.

"I should tell you that he was frightened."

"Of winning the lottery?"

"Walter Benjamin has a wife who has a brother who insists that the ticket is his."

"His?"

"He claims his sister bought it for him and that Walter and Peter have stolen it."

"And that is false?"

Had she not considered that O'Reilly might be telling her a story? Apparently not. Still, I found her naiveté engaging.

"How does one get to be coroner?"

"It was the biggest mistake I ever made. I was flattered when they offered to put me on the ballot. My practice was just on the verge of being established."

Of course she was a medical doctor. Her specialty was knees.

"Knees?"

"Replacements."

She crossed her legs and despite the desk between us it was clear that her own knees were irreplaceable.

"All these dead bodies." She made a face. "Ish."

"That's my nickname. Short for Ishmael."

"How on earth did you get a name like that?"

"The deed was done long before I could do anything about it."

She tossed her ponytail. She wanted to get back to O'Reilly. Her manner in my office earlier, her apparent interest in me, was all aimed at Peter O'Reilly.

"I'll need a retainer."

"I'm a doctor, not a dentist."

I explained. She wrote a check which I put in my shirt pocket with the five and five ones, pens, pencils—everything but the lottery ticket that had briefly pressed reassuringly against my breast.

"When is the last time you saw him?"

"This morning." She lifted her chin as if daring my moral censure. "When he left."

I had loathed O'Reilly before. Now I hated him.

"I'll get on it."

In the car, I called Brunswick again.

"Turn yourself in, Slattery."

"Listen, I can tell you who put the knife in the back of Walter Benjamin."

"I would prefer that you make your confession in person. Your fingerprints were all over his wallet."

I waited. Of course he did not mention my fingerprints on the knife. I hadn't even known it was there until Brunswick flipped the body.

"The man you are looking for is Peter O'Reilly."

I shut down the connection, decided against calling Gwen, and headed for my office.

6

When I got to the office, I found Gwen seated in my chair, to which she was tied. Her eyes widened over the gag in her mouth as I came in, and she began to nod her head frantically. There was a faint whooshing sound and then something crashed down on my head. Lights flared, burst, went out. And so did I.

Consciousness crept through the crevices of my aching head. My cheek was pressed against the carpet. My hands, I discovered, when I tried to move them, were tied behind my back. I tried to lift my head, but the muscles that make this an easy maneuver for turtles were, in my case, unused.

A simple test told me that my ankles too were tied. An involuntary groan escaped me.

"Ish? Are you all right?"

It was Gwen. No answer seemed required. Another groan sufficed. Someone kicked me in the side. To escape further kicks I rolled away and ended on my back, a turtle indeed. The upside-down face of an attractive young man looked down at me.

"Peter O'Reilly?" I guessed.

"Where is that ticket, Slattery?"

Ah. So Gwen had resisted his threats. But obviously her gag had been removed. Or perhaps she had chewed through it. I at least was free to talk.

"Untie me and we will discuss the matter like civilized men."

He circled me so that the top of his head was to the north, as was mine. "Does that mean you have it?"

"It means I may be of help in locating it. I have spoken with Horace Munn."

"That thief!"

"Precisely what he said about you."

He kicked me in the side again.

"Stop that!" Gwen cried.

"Untie me or we won't be able to get out of here before the police arrive."

He laughed, or tried to. A frown brought his brows together. "And where would we be going?"

For answer, I waggled my tied wrists at him. Mention of the police had been inspired. No wonder. It occurred to me that I was lying approximately where Walter Benjamin had lain before shuffling off this mortal coil. Peter O'Reilly decided to act. He pulled a knife from a leather pouch worn like a shoulder holster inside his suit jacket. The memory of

181

Benjamin and the sight of that knife did not give me peace of mind. He crouched beside me, then hesitated.

"You're bluffing."

"But you don't know for sure."

"If you are . . ." he began, menacingly.

It was Gwen who completed the thought. "You'll do to him what you did to Benjamin."

"Shut up," I pleaded.

"What did I do to Benjamin?" His mouth remained open. He looked from me to Gwen and back again. "Was Walter here?"

"Yes, and he left in a body bag," Gwen said.

"Please shut up, Gwen."

O'Reilly's lower lip folded outward, and he shook his head. "That's bunk."

What an actor. And what a time waster. Why should he care what Gwen and I knew about the late Walter Benjamin and how he had got that way? But I was puzzled at his reaction. He had reacted to my lie that the police were on the way like a guilty man. Now he was crouched beside me, running his thumb along the edge of his knife, seemingly concerned that we not think ill of him. Just because he had tied up Gwen and knocked me over the head before doing the same to me, he apparently didn't want us to think him capable of harming anyone.

"Cut me loose," I begged.

He did. With one deft movement of the knife he set my wrists free. I would like to say that I immediately grabbed him by the lapels, shook the knife from his hand, rolled on top him and began to beat his head against the floor. In the real world, I said, "Thanks. My ankles?"

"Me next," Gwen begged. O'Reilly and I ignored her. I had to keep from looking into the large liquid unforgiving eyes of Ayn Rand. O'Reilly cut my ankles free. He actually helped me to my feet.

"Are the cops really coming?"

"I'm surprised they aren't already here."

"Ish, darling, make him untie me," Gwen pleaded.

O'Reilly stopped and looked at her, then at me. "She your wife?"

"Ha."

"Lying won't fool him, Ish."

O'Reilly said to me in considerate tones, "Let me see your wrists."

I held them out for him to inspect the damage he had done. In a quince he had tied them again with the rope taken from my ankles.

"Hey!"

"Sit down so I can do your ankles."

This suggestion was the more persuasive because he had his knife pressed against my stomach. He pushed me backward, I hit the wall and slid down it into a sitting position. He tied my ankles. Then he went behind the desk and put a gag around the struggling Gwen's mouth. She tried to give him a two-footed kick but without success.

"Here's the plan," O'Reilly said, and I didn't like the nervousness in his voice. "She's going with me, as security. When the cops find you, tell them Horace Munn was here. Got that? Horace Munn. When they let you go, you get that ticket. You better have it when I call you."

Whereupon he pushed the wheeled chair to which Gwen was tied around the desk, across the office and out the door. I heard the elevator open and then close. Silence.

Most of us lead lives of quiet desperation, never pausing to wonder why we are rushing mindlessly about. Moments of meditation seem never to come. The unexamined life may not be worth living, but it is the only life we live. Tied up in my office, I had a welcome opportunity to reflect a bit on the great questions which ever trouble the human heart, if we only give them entry. What does it all mean? How does the free man differ from one tied up in his office, I mean really differ? Or, as someone must have said, Oh what a worldwide web we weave when first we practice to deceive. Why in hell had I told O'Reilly the police were coming?

No need to chronicle my efforts to free myself from my bonds. The ropes seemed only to tighten when I tried to loosen them. The sun grew brighter at the window as it began it slow descent over the western horizon. My stomach rumbled and I fought off fond thoughts of Weenie's where foods rich in cholesterol were to be had, and enervating drink until the cows come home.

It grew dark outside. The suppressed sobbing was mine, but does a tree falling in the forest make noise if it is not heard? There were no witnesses to my shame. "Let me see your wrists," he had said, and like an idiot I had held them out. Why? Because at the moment it had seemed to be me and O'Reilly against Gwen. I had imagined the two of us going, leaving the tied up Gwen to her own devices. I was filled with remorse. In my weakened condition I felt tenderness toward Gwen. What a great little girl she was. Not much meat on her bones but no muscle in her head. Where had O'Reilly taken her? I might have feared for her virtue but in that at least she was safe. O'Reilly would find her less concupiscible than the chair she was tied to. Poor girl.

The office was illumined now by the street lamps below. I thought of Horace Munn and wondered if he were still at Weenie's, waiting for word from me. That was absurd, of course. Had he played me for a fool? Had his sister, poor

Walter Benjamin's widow? And, unkindest cut of all, had Marlys Frigosso? Although O'Reilly had been made nervous by my mention of the police, he seemed genuinely ignorant of what had happened to Walter Benjamin, his partner if not his friend. And the beau of Marlys Frigosso. Ah, break, my heart. My thoughts came round to Horace Munn.

Interlude

There are an enlightened few, among them Arthur Conan Doyle and myself, who are convinced that men possess latent extra-sensory powers, that some few of us can learn of another world just out of reach of our senses. I have long counted myself a member of that minuscule minority of the race. Sometimes, without provocation, street scenes in Cairo will appear to my mind's eye as vividly as if I were an eyewitness. The first time, this happened, I turned off the Travel Channel and sat shivering in my chair. But courage returned and I shut my eyes tightly and sent thoughts up to whatever satellite awaited them. And I was answered. I had the distinct sensation of someone nibbling on my left earlobe. A quite substantial hand mussed my hair. And then I was being tickled mercilessly. I rose to escape, but Gwen pursued me, her fingers busy at my rib cage.

"I was having an out-of-body experience," I said gravely. "You broke the spell."

She pushed me back into the chair and clambered onto my lap. By constantly twisting my head I managed to avoid her hungry lips.

"Ish, we haven't had a client in months."

"Think of it as vacation time."

"The till is empty, the checking account has zeroed out. I am going in search of a client."

"I will not have you selling yourself."

Small wiry people are stronger than they look. Gwen packed

*a helluva punch. I was gasping for air when she turned at the
door. "Why don't you try another out-of-body experience."*

"With you, that will be the only way," I said meanly.

"You're out of your mind already."

*The door slammed. That was Wednesday, the day before
Walter Benjamin called. Never underestimate the power of the
human mind.*

All this is prelude for the arrival of Horace Munn on
Friday morning. Having thought of Horace Munn, having
arrived at his name as if by a process of elimination, I was not
surprised to hear the elevator door open. My heart leapt in
hope, however—in hope and apprehension. The tread I heard
could only be that of Horace Munn. And then the door burst
open, the light was turned on and Horace Munn looked down
at me with an expression I shall not attempt to describe.

"Good God, what's happened?"

"I'm all tied up."

I might have been telling him that business was good.
But Munn was a man of direct action. In a moment my
hands and feet were free. He helped me to my feet and into
a chair.

"Tell me everything."

Should I have felt fear? As I lay sighing on my office
floor, my one consolation was that the lottery ticket that explained the events of the day was safe in my safe, and only I
knew it. Well, Gwen and I. So long as that secret was kept,
all misadventures and pains of the day were well worth the
candle. So I told Horace Munn everything, in my fashion.

"I had been in pursuit of leads to the missing ticket, I had
spoken to your sister, I consulted with Dr. Frigosso . . ."

"The coroner?"

"You know her?"

"Peter O'Reilly is nuts about her."

"As any sane man would be."

"Did you talk with O'Reilly?"

"I returned to my office, came through that door and was suddenly attacked from behind. I was bludgeoned and lost consciousness. When I came to I was as you found me."

"O'Reilly," he growled.

"Why would you think so?"

Munn had been pacing the floor, listening to my highly edited account, but now he stopped and wheeled on me.

"Is anything missing?"

I looked around, my eyes grazing the arrogant countenance of Ayn Rand, but going on. "Everything looks as usual. I would have to check, of course."

"Why would he have come here? Because he thinks Walter Benjamin brought you the ticket."

"Walter Benjamin came here on the brink of death. We did not exchange two words before he expired."

News of Benjamin's death had reached Weenie's and Horace Munn had a fanciful version of what had happened. Benjamin was assaulted in the elevator, pushed out on my floor, and staggered into my office. His assailant went back down in the elevator and disappeared.

"To think I might have run into the murderer if I hadn't taken the stairs."

I shook my head at the wondrous ways of the world.

"I was following him. I followed him into this building and when he took the elevator I took the stairs."

"Why were you hiding in the closet?"

"I was waiting for him to come out of your office. Then all hell broke loose and I stepped into the closet. Filthy place."

"If only you had followed him into that elevator."

"But why was he coming here?"

"We'll never know."

7

Free at last, I did not, as romantic readers might expect, turn immediately to rescuing Gwen. For one thing, the carefully censored tale I had told Munn eliminated Gwen from the picture. My account of being knocked out as I entered my office had not mentioned Peter O'Reilly either, although Munn had surmised that O'Reilly was my assailant.

I parted with Munn on the walk outside my building and then went swiftly to Weenie's where I ordered the ER Platter, a heap of noxious foodstuffs soaked with lethal and tasty sauces. ER? Well, to forgive's divine. Think about it. Weenie did for a long time when Gwen said it. So ask her.

Thoughts of Gwen pestered me as I consoled the inner man with the ER Platter. Was she still as I had last seen her, bound, gagged, a prisoner? But first things first. Along with my meal, I digested the events of the day.

A rapid review teased a central question from the lot. Had Brunswick taken my advice and gone in search of Peter O'Reilly? When I left Weenie's, I set off, still driving Gwen's vehicle, and called police headquarters as I wove through traffic.

"He works days," a grumpy voice told me.

"You got his home number?"

"Who's this?"

"I just got out of prison and I want to get even with the cop who sent me there."

"Stay on the line, will you?"

I hung up before he could start tracing the call. And then

I was at my destination, Primrose Lanes. It was here that Brunswick was known to put off the cares of the day by bowling a few lines before he drank himself insensible in the bar and was taken home by his designated driver, himself.

Primrose Lanes was a time warp. The air was dense with smoke, redolent of alcohol, echoing with the authoritative roar of balls hitting pins. Here men were men, and women retained the strategically subservient air that had enabled them to rule the world before feminism ruined everything. A blowsy redhead who had let herself go, figure-wise, seemed to be offering the cornucopia of her blouse to Brunswick as she leaned toward him. Her lips were moist with beer, her eyes danced with promise. She was not, needless to say, Mrs. Brunswick. The Junoesque redhead was Ashley Mountain, sole proprietor of the Primrose since the mysterious death of her husband. On the day he closed the case, Brunswick had drowned his sorrows at the Primrose and became unable to drive himself. As if to show him she bore no grudges because her husband's death was now a dead issue, Ashley took the dejected detective home. It had been the beginning of a long alliance.

"Slattery," Ashley Mountain said, sneering.

"Check his ID," Brunswick advised.

"Gwen Probst has been kidnapped by Peter O'Reilly."

"Tell the police."

"You're the police."

"I'm off duty. It's Friday night, for crying out loud."

"Scram," Ashley said. She had stood and punctuated her advice with a swift movement of her hip that sent me reeling. I crashed against the ball rack, steadied myself and then stood with a bowling ball dangling from my thumb.

"I know who killed Walter Benjamin, Brunswick."

"This isn't the place, Slattery."

"Walter Benjamin?" Ashley said, interested. "Isn't that Letitia's husband?"

"You know her?" I asked. "Walter's her late husband."

"She and Peter bowl here sometimes."

"Beat it, Slattery," Brunswick growled. "The sun is over the yardarm. Give your mind a rest."

He lifted his beer mug to his face. I fought my way through the crowd but before I could leave a hand gripped my arm. Ashley.

"Come into my office."

The walls were filled with photos of celebrities, inscribed with overblown dedications to Ashley. "They're from the place I had in Chicago. A long time ago." Her voice had dropped to a whisper.

"Hardly that," I suggested gallantly.

She came close and I could feel her enormous breasts pressing against me. There were tears in her eyes as she looked into mine.

"Peter O'Reilly is my son."

"Tell me about it."

Ah, the sinuous route that DNA takes, moving from generation to generation, forming previously unknown combinations, passing on some traits of the parents, one long twisted chain reaching back to Adam and Eve. Ashley's story was trite but nonetheless moving. She had fallen in love with a singer who accompanied himself on the piano, Owen O'Reilly. He had been booked into her place, one thing led to another, she tried to persuade him to get off the circuit and settle in permanently with her. But the song of the open road was his theme. He went off, never to be seen again, but he had left behind, under Ashley's heart, a flesh and blood memento of his sojourn.

"When I saw he was a boy I named him Peter."

"Of course."

"I gave him everything. I set him up in business."

"With Walter Benjamin."

"You keep mentioning him."

"He died in my office yesterday morning."

"Dear God."

"Stabbed in the back."

She put her hands on my arms; the pressure of her breasts and the beery aroma of her breath would have been too much for a lesser man. She slapped my hand away. "Listen. You're a detective. Find Peter. Find him and bring him here."

"Why don't you just call and ask him over?"

"You know why."

She looked at me significantly. I nodded.

"This could be expensive."

Then and there, she plopped down at her desk, pulled out a checkbook and scribbled rapidly. She handed the torn-out check to me. Five thousand dollars. I folded it and put it in my shirt pocket.

"I will have your son here before the night is out or my name isn't Ishmael Slattery."

The dramatic effect of this was momentarily lessened by the opening of the door. The roar of the bar became audible and then Peter O'Reilly slipped in. When he saw me, he stopped.

"Go to your mother, son," I said gently.

Patting my shirt pocket, I bowed to Ashley and left.

8

Never had such a sum seemed less significant. I directed myself to my office. What was a mere five thousand dollars compared to the worth of the lottery ticket in my office safe? Best to take possession of it now, before Gwen was freed and beat me to the punch. I tried not to dwell on Ashley Mountain's revelation. Peter O'Reilly, her son. The son she had set up in business with Walter Benjamin. Partners not friends, who had pooled their money to buy lottery tickets. Doubtless they had bought a ticket or tickets for Wednesday's lottery. Whether the winning ticket was among them, or had been purchased for Horace Munn by his sister, Letitia Benjamin, was the bone of contention. But Walter Benjamin was now dead. Ashley referred to the deceased as if he were the estranged husband of Letitia and said that Peter and Letitia sometimes bowled together. When Peter suddenly appeared in Ashley's office I recognized a cue for a dramatic exit. Had I remained, I would have wanted to punish the son who had tied me up and beaten me.

I wished I had asked him where he had left Gwen.

What is so deserted as an office building at night? I parked in the basement garage, and took the staircase to my floor. I emerged huffing on 4 and after gathering my forces proceeded down the hall to my office.

The door was locked. Why did that surprise me? I reeled my keys from my pocket, twirled my key chain once or twice, let go and plucked the relevant key from the bunch as it descended. But before I could get it into the lock, the door opened and Gwen looked out at me.

"Gwen! Thank God you're safe. I've been frantic."

I took her bony body into my arms so she could not read my eyes and know me for the cowardly liar I was.

"What did you do with the lottery ticket?"

I looked into her honest, inquiring eyes and suddenly my legs turned to jelly. She steadied me and led me to the chair behind the desk.

"You brought it back," I observed.

"I'll tell you about that later. Where's the ticket?"

"Gwen, as God is my judge I did not remove it from the safe."

"But only you and I know the combination."

"Has the safe been damaged?"

She pushed aside the portrait of Ayn Rand. A few deft movements of her wrist and the door swung open. There were no signs of jimmying, explosives, or anything else. The safe was empty. I wanted to cry. I did cry. Gwen gathered me to her and it was like being hugged by a coat rack.

"In a way I'm glad," she murmured.

"Don't say that!"

"Ish, what is money, what is wealth? Have you ever known a happy rich man?"

"I've known a lot of unhappy poor men, among whom I now include myself."

"We probably couldn't have cashed it anyway."

"There you're wrong. I would have been the last live or unjailed claimant. Who are my rivals? Benjamin is dead. Peter O'Reilly probably killed him. Horace Munn tried to confiscate a ticket that was not his. Who's left with clean hands but me?"

"You did wash afterward?" She had heard me stop down the hall before coming to the office.

"And before. If you knew where I have been."

"Tell me all about it, Ish."

She was seated on my lap. Anchorites might have devised such a remedy for concupiscence. Still her hair smelt lovely. I buried my nose in it. And then I told her my tale.

"Peter O'Reilly is the son of Ashley Mountain, proprietress of the Primrose Lanes. They were involved in a touching reunion when I left them."

"I thought you said Peter O'Reilly is the murderer."

"Even murderers have mothers."

"Have you convinced Brunswick?"

"Ha. I suspect he is living in sin with Ashley Mountain. No, I will get no help from him. I am on my own, Gwen. The way I like it. Slattery against the world."

"Slattery and Probst."

"Just so."

The safe was closed, the portrait of Ayn Rand swung back into place, I felt as miserable as I had forty-eight hours ago when I sat at this very desk and drank myself into oblivion. But I was a different Ishmael Slattery now, fresh from a wild roller coaster ride that had taken me to high hopes of unimaginable wealth and then plunged me into the slough of despond, poor once more. I was as steel tested in the fire. I would avenge myself for the foul murder committed in my office Thursday morning. I voiced all this in Churchillian tones I will not try to capture in cold print. I could feel Gwen thrill to my eloquence.

"Go get him, Ish," she urged.

"Who?"

"The killer."

"Of course." But it was that winning lottery ticket I meant to get.

"What can I do?" Gwen asked.

"Get a good night's rest."

"But what about you?"

"Don't worry about me."

I expected resistance. I was prepared for Gwen to insist on sticking with me through thick and thin, making a pest of herself. When I have narrowed the field and am moving in on my man, I do not want the encumbrance of a woman. To my enormous surprise Gwen accepted this. She planted an impulsive kiss on my forehead, got to her feet and walked to a point three feet from the door where she turned to look at me. A loving and admiring smile took possession of her thin lips. She raised one hand, wiggled its fingers and then was gone.

I waited, listening intently, but I heard her footsteps recede, heard the elevator open and close and then the silence deepened. Alone at last.

Of course I knew what had happened. Gwen had broken under the threat of violence and opened the safe for Peter O'Reilly. That young man very likely had the winning ticket on his person when he showed up at his mother's office at Primrose Lanes. The question remained: how to get that ticket back. I had to count on O'Reilly's unwillingness to act before morning. I must return to Primrose Lanes, either to find O'Reilly there or to learn where he might have gone. Would he have told his mother of his bonanza?

The phone rang and I jumped. I looked at it, willing it into silence, but it continued to ring at programmed intervals. Finally, to shut it up, I answered.

"I knew you were there, Slattery."

"Horace Munn?"

"You were going to call me."

"Weenie's number has been busy."

"Should I come up there?"

"No! No. I think I am onto it now, Munn."

"I told you it was O'Reilly. Get him, get the ticket, and get paid."

I smiled at the simplicity of the non-professional mind. Of course he had had some reason to think O'Reilly had stolen the ticket. But that was this morning, when the ticket was secure in my office safe. Now it was gone and I had professional reason to think that Peter O'Reilly had frightened

Gwen into opening the safe. Or cajoled her? Worked on her feminine fragility, that irrational amenability to the mendacious male that characterizes the honest half of the species? I tried to dismiss this scenario, but could not. I recalled the good looking O'Reilly and juxtaposed him to the spare and sinewy Gwen. On the other hand, she represented access to millions. What might a man not endure for stakes such as those?

Whatever, or however, Gwen must have opened the safe. No wonder she had slunk off to her apartment and left me to my own devices. She was ashamed to be in my presence. O'Reilly had the ticket he had been pursuing all day.

"You may be right," I said to Munn. "Still want me to call you at Weenie's?"

"When do they close?"

"Two in the morning."

"After two call me at home." He gave me a number which I wrote in air and then blew away.

"Right."

I replaced the phone, stood, and tucked my shirt tail in. Then I set out for Primrose Lanes on a mission that would likely break a mother's heart.

9

"Slattery," a voice whispered as I came into the basement garage. I turned to see Marlys Frigosso peering around a pillar. "Are you alone?"

"As you see."

"Come here." Stouter hearts might have resisted this appeal. Her voice trembled, her eyes were doe-like in the ill-lit garage. Steel filings never were drawn more helplessly to a magnet than I was drawn to Dr. Frigosso. Only when I was inches from her did she reveal that she was holding a gun. Her expression changed.

"What have you done with Peter?"

"Done with him? I'm trying to find him."

"He said he was going to your office. That was yesterday afternoon. I've been frantic, waiting for him to call."

"Oh, he came to see me all right. He tied and gagged me and he kidnapped my assistant."

"That—thin girl?"

"Looks can be deceiving."

"What do you mean?"

"A gentleman never tells."

"Did you tell the police?"

"About her voracious habits? It's not against the law, you know. Not anymore."

Frigosso grew impatient. "Tell them she had been kidnapped!"

"I have talked with the police, yes." I thought of Brunswick, lolling at his table in the bar of Primrose Lanes, lips moist with liquor, eyes bleary with dissipation. Support your local police.

"I'm coming with you, Slattery."

In other circumstances this would have been a pleasing prospect indeed. It wasn't altogether displeasing then. And, after all, she had the gun and was punctuating her determination with flourishes of the weapon.

"My insurance won't cover you."

She nudged my side with the gun and I yelped. "That's where Peter kicked me."

"I don't believe that."

"Well, maybe it was a little higher."

"We'll go in my car."

A good idea. Gwen's vehicle was gone, and my own

would still be low on gas. Frigosso drove a luxury car made by third-world immigrants along the Rhine. It was low, long and powerful, but it required acrobatic skills to get into. Once one's bottom sank into the leather upholstery, however, the charms of the vehicle began to make themselves felt. I followed her instructions, feeling as if I were at the controls of the Stealth. When I turned the key, the dashboard came alive in a variety of basic colors, flashing, bar graphs, digital read-outs.

"Is it on?"

"Of course."

The motor was noiseless. I eased the shift into drive and the car moved across the oil stained floor like a cat advancing on a bird's nest. Up the ramp and onto the street. The car seemed an extension of my arms as I retraced my route to Primrose Lanes.

"Why are you stopping here?"

"Not an hour ago I left Peter here with the woman he loves."

She gave me a mocking laugh. "Your assistant?"

The bowling lanes were shut down, but there were lights in the bar. Someone was playing the piano. Peter O'Reilly. Frigosso and I stopped in the shadowed entry to the bar and listened to Peter play and sing, his words seeming to rise like smoke up the cone of light that fell from a ceiling fixture. My memory for music is terrible and my ear is tin. I do remember that the words he sang claimed that he was rich as Rockefeller. Was this the triumphant crowing of a man who had beaten the opposition to the winning lottery ticket?

Marlys Frigosso drifted into the bar and collapsed at a small table, enthralled by the entertainer. I had not moved when a hand was laid on my arm. I turned. It was Ashley, her eyes swimming with tears.

"God bless you," she said.

I sneezed.

"Only that woman can wean him from Letitia."

This lovely sentence parsed into: (a) Frigosso would be
the salvation of Ashley's son Peter, (b) Peter had been mis-
behaving with Letitia, once wife and now widow of his slain
partner Walter Benjamin, and (c) the implication that
Ashley did not realize her son had killed Benjamin, kidnapped
my partner, tied and gagged myself, and importuned Gwen
into opening the office safe and handing over a lottery ticket
worth enough to pay a major league pitcher for half a
season.

"Letitia is a widow now."

"Sure she is. The old-fashioned way."

I thought of the matronly sister of Horace Munn. Only
the mother of her lover could think ill of her.

"Has Peter said anything to you since he arrived?"

"Peter? He's always been a chatterbox."

At that moment a disheveled miserable figure stumbled
out of the men's room and blinked his eyes against the glare
from a twenty-watt ceiling bulb.

"Brunswick," I said, steadying the lieutenant. "There's
something you must do."

"I just did."

"Do you still have your weapon?"

"What kind of question is that?"

I pulled him away from Ashley and whispered rapidly in
his ear. I told him everything, almost, but more than
enough to get him to act. He tried his best to follow what I
was saying. From time to time he glanced into the bar at
Peter singing in his smoky cone of light. Brunswick broke
free, shaking his head.

"Not tonight, Slattery. It would spoil the party. Give me a call in the morning. Late morning. Come on, sweetie." He took Ashley's arm and the two of them careened among the tables to a place near the piano.

Tomorrow morning. I would hold him to that. It was time I wrapped this up. While I had possession of the lottery ticket, there was reason for prolonging the investigation, if only to divert suspicion from myself. But now, poor as a church mouse again, I hungered and thirsted for justice.

10

For purposes of narrative efficiency I like to gather all the elements of the puzzle in my office when I pierce through the mystery of events and reveal the underlying causes. Brunswick had said morning, but it was nearly noon before he untangled himself from the arms of Morpheus or whoever and answered the phone. Anxious to get some Alka-Seltzer, he agreed to everything. The whole cast would be present in my office at three that afternoon. Gwen smiled her admiration as I put down the phone.

"Ish, you're indescribable."

"I never felt worse in my life."

"Just when you are going to reveal the murderer of Walter Benjamin?"

"Oh that. Gwen, we could have been rich."

"You know I have money." She was a heiress, I mustn't forget that. But the thought of being filthy rich myself, of having been so close to it, made me want to weep.

"What's mine is yours, Ish."

She meant well.

"After we're married . . ."

I took her in my arms to shut her up. When I released

her, her eyes were half closed, her lips parted. She sighed.

"I must think," I told her. "I must get ready."

"Of course."

I closed my eyes and tipped back in my chair. A mistake. It kept going back, spilling me onto the floor. I shook off Gwen's help and went to the couch where I curled into the fetal position.

Horace Munn arrived with his sister. "I hope this won't take long. Walter's wake is this evening." Letitia looked around my office as if she would like to do a thorough cleaning job. Brunswick brought Ashley and Peter, and Marlys Frigosso breezed in, tossing her saucy ponytail, with eyes for Peter alone. I was surprised when Weenie came in and was given a chair in the back by Gwen.

"I asked him," she explained.

"Get on with it, Slattery," Brunswick groused.

Well, these were always difficult moments for him. I was more than happy to do his work for Brunswick, but I would have been happier if there were any prospect of being decently paid for it. But who was my client? I had taken token retainers from Benjamin, Munn, Frigosso and something more sizeable from Ashley Mountain. In the last case, I had fulfilled my assignment. I patted my shirt pocket; her check was still there. Maybe I would invest it in lottery tickets.

"On Thursday morning," I began, "a wounded man came to that door, entered this office and collapsed. There!" I pointed and Letitia moved her feet. "He gave me a lottery ticket that contained winning numbers for the previous night's drawing. He entrusted it to me and I put it in a safe place."

"You had that ticket when I first talked to you?" Horace

Munn's great hands opened and closed as once they had on the neck of Peter O'Reilly. I waved this interruption away. "When we first talked, you did not know that the man you accused of theft had died minutes before in my office."

"You never told me."

"Elementary strategy," Gwen said, from her post at the side of the room. "Please don't interrupt Mr. Slattery."

"At your instructions, Horace Munn, I went in pursuit of Peter O'Reilly. Targets of opportunity along the way were Letitia Benjamin and Marlys Frigosso."

"Of course you had not known previously of their attachment to your quarry."

I let Gwen's observation waste its sweetness on the charged expectant air in the office. Such interventions were the price I paid for our partnership. I went on.

"In the event, Peter O'Reilly came to me."

Gwen came and stood beside me. "With his customary modesty, Mr. Slattery is skimming over the heart of the matter. The heart of the matter is of course the winning lottery ticket."

"The murder it led to trumps everything else," I said.

"Here is that ticket," Gwen said, plucking a colorful piece of pasteboard from the recesses of her unnecessary bra. Everyone in the office leaned toward her. Their expressions were so many studies in the capital sins. Would Gwen's theatrical gesture work? No one could know that the ticket she held was not the winner. How could it be? That had been stolen from its unjust possessor, your humble servant. "May I?" Gwen said, looking to me.

I nodded and waved my hand, the gesture conveying both permission and non-complicity.

"As Mr. Slattery says, this ticket was crucial. Horace Munn says that he asked his sister to purchase a ticket for him. Did you do that, Mrs. Benjamin?"

A slight nod of her wild-haired head.

"And you, Peter O'Reilly, you bought a ticket with joint ownership with Walter Benjamin."

"I did. And I gave it to Walter to hold."

"So we have two tickets. Both of them in the Benjamin household. Shall I continue, Ishmael?"

"Do."

"Horace Munn claims he was informed by his sister that she had bought for him the winning ticket. She does not corroborate his story. Who is telling the truth, the brother or sister?"

Letitia moved away from her huge brother, whose scowl was becoming fierce.

"In either case, the winning ticket was in the Benjamin household. On the fateful morning my partner has mentioned, the late Walter Benjamin as his last act on earth brought this ticket to this office. Mr. Slattery locked it in the office safe. And there it remained until . . ."

"Until you," I cried, pointing at Peter O'Reilly, "came here, overpowered Miss Probst, hit me over the head . . ." I ran out of indignant breath. Gwen patted my arm and asked if she should continue. I nodded.

"Mr. Slattery is understandably overcome with emotion. And he rightly surmised that the ticket had been removed from the safe as a result of Peter O'Reilly's visit. Peter O'Reilly pushed me out of this office tied, as he thought, to that chair. Actually, I had freed myself minutes before we left the office. Once we were in the elevator, I overpowered him . . ."

"She jumped me from behind," Peter piped.

"I left him in the elevator, having put the office chair in a safe place, and spent the next hours acquainting myself with the habits of all of you." Her eyes traveled around the office from face to face.

"I learned of the liaison between Lieutenant Brunswick and Ashley Mountain. I learned that any idea that Peter O'Reilly was enthralled with Dr. Frigosso was entirely in her mind."

"He reprogrammed my hard drive," the coroner wailed.

"But his heart belonged to another. Peter had told his mother of the winning ticket."

"A perfectly normal thing," Ashley said.

"But he led you to believe the winning ticket was his."

"Who can prove otherwise?" Peter O'Reilly said.

"The man who could have has been killed," I cried. I was getting sick of that damned ticket. We had a murder to account for.

"Mr. Slattery indicated that he had put the ticket in the safe. Actually he entrusted the task to me. Even though he was watching, I managed to palm the ticket before closing the safe door. I put it in my bosom. That is why, when under duress, I opened the safe for Peter O'Reilly it was empty. Little did he suspect that the object of his desire was on my person."

"You had the winning ticket all along?" I looked at her, half in admiration, half in anger.

"No. The ticket Walter Benjamin brought you was not the winning ticket."

At football games a missed extra point will deflate the crowd and a collective sigh accompanies the seeming sinking into itself of the vast throng. So, all proportions guarded, was it in my office.

"Then where the hell is it?" Horace Munn asked.

Gwen let a silence build, then she turned. "Why don't you tell us, Letitia."

"I don't know what you mean."

Gwen plucked another colorful piece of pasteboard from her bra. "I found this in your sewing basket, Letitia. This is the ticket you bought for your brother, isn't it?"

Letitia Benjamin looked serenely about her, saying nothing. Horace stared at her open-mouthed.

"When your husband, under the impression you had given him that he held the winning ticket, set out for this office, you followed him. And you plunged this into his back as he entered the elevator downstairs. Weenie?"

"I was out for a smoke and I saw her come here," Weenie said.

Gwen pointed to Brunswick who held up a plastic bag in which the knife taken from Benjamin's back was visible.

"That matches the steak knives in your kitchen, Letitia. What was your plan? You were rid of your husband, but how would you placate your brother?"

"We would have been long gone," Letitia cried, suddenly animated. "We would have been in Antigua, in the sun, on the sand." Her happy voice was broken by her sob.

"We," Gwen repeated. "Meaning you and Peter."

"I know nothing," Peter O'Reilly cried. He had moved next to Frigosso and tried to take her hand. She snatched it free and half turned from him.

"You said we would run away together," Letitia cried. "It was for you that I stole that ticket. It was for you that . . ."

"That you killed your husband," I completed. "Take her away, Brunswick. Take them all away."

Gwen, turning to me, began to clap and the applause was taken up, not with the wholehearted enthusiasm my performance justified, but acceptable enough. Brunswick led the struggling Letitia away, the identified murderer protesting that she had to go to her husband's wake.

Weenie hurried out and Peter went off with his mother. In the doorway, Marlys Frigosso looked wistfully back at me, and then she too was gone. Gwen leaned over me and pressed something into my pocket. A lottery ticket.

11

Gwen vetoed my suggestion that we repair to Longboat Key to enjoy the fruits of our efforts.

"Florida in August? Are you mad?"

And so it was in a modest villa on the Upper Peninsula that my partner and I sat on a veranda looking at loons diving at the lake waters while a ruby red sun set slowly in the west.

"There was no winning ticket," I said miserably.

Letitia had lied to her brother in the hope that he would do in her husband. She lied to Peter too, seeking to lure him away from the flippant ponytail of the comely coroner. One life had been taken and the emotions of others sent careening from high to low to high to low. Walter Benjamin's insurance was meant to make up for the imaginary millions won in the lottery. I sat on the veranda, recalling my efforts, recalling the hopes and fears, the humiliation of being bound and gagged by Peter O'Reilly. That young man had decided to become his mother's partner and croon away the evenings in the bar of Primrose Lanes. Letitia had been arraigned and was destined for a long vacation at public expense.

"Vanity of vanities," I sighed. "All is vanity."

"That's catchy," Gwen said, plopping down on my lap. I embraced her. To what serves mortal beauty? What is a little extra flesh here, voluptuous padding there, the promise of sensual riot? Gwen would have been safe from a motorcycle gang, but she was the bird in hand. I stroked her feathered hair.

"Life is a lottery," I intoned.

"Oh, shut up." And she brazenly pressed her lips to mine. She got to her feet. "Now I'm going to take a nap. For just half an hour. Call me, Ishmael."

ABOUT THE AUTHOR

Author and editor RALPH MCINERNY has long been acknowledged as one of the most vital voices in lay Catholic activities in America. He is co-founder and co-publisher of *CRISIS*, a widely read journal of Catholic opinion, while finding time to teach Medieval Studies and Philosophy at Notre Dame University and write several series of mystery novels, including a legal mystery series featuring lawyer Andrew Bloom and a more recent series set at Notre Dame itself. His most famous creation, *The Father Dowling Mysteries*, ran on network television for several seasons, and can now be seen on cable. For his achievements in the mystery field, he was awarded the Anthony Award for Lifetime Achievement in 1993. Scholars are rarely entertainers, but he has been both for many years.